TH.
BOOK

Robert Ryan

Cover Design by www.damonza.com

ISBN: 9781093445299
(print edition)

Trotting Fox Press

Contents

1. A Magician of Power

Unferth sat still, a mask over his features. A king should at least *look* as though events moved at his control, but he worried that even the guise of orderly rule had slipped away from him.

Frustration made him want to smash his hand against the table. But he could not, for it would only prove that he was angry and therefore *not* in perfect control. This fed the anger that burned inside him even more. And that anger was red hot, raging and desperate to be unleashed.

But deeper inside, in his innermost thoughts that he shared with no one, was something colder than ice. It was the thing that troubled him most. Fear.

It was an ever-present whisper. It was the voice of doubt. It was the rasp of steel blades drawn in a nightmare from which he could not wake. Fear. It sent a chill through him that nothing ever warmed. And unlike the fear of most men that was formless and vague, his had a specific name. Brand.

Brand haunted him. Even as a child, having escaped the killing of his parents, Brand had been like a sore that would not heal. If only he had been there that night, if only he had died as he was supposed to, the world would be a better place. Unferth knew it, knew that the sun would have shone upon him and he would have ruled both the Callenor and the Duthenor in a noontide of glory.

But Brand was a shadow upon him, and the shadow lengthened year by year. And now came this. A final insult like a crack that could widen and destroy the life he had worked so hard for. Why did other men have it so easy while he must he fight tooth and claw like an animal for what was his?

His fury boiled over. Despite the look of calm he knew he should maintain, he smashed his hand against the table anyway. The sudden noise stilled everything about him. The hall became quiet, and his counselors turned surprised gazes upon him. Fools! They did not understand. They never would.

He spoke slowly, showing as much restraint as he could.

"Why do you all debate this? Horta has told you what happened. Brand defeated the force sent against him. Outnumbered, he found a way to grasp victory." That he must say those words humbled him, and the voice of doubt in his mind was more than a whisper now. "We'll not beat him by debating among ourselves. You can be sure that already he moves against us. What shall we do? *That* is the question we must answer, and swiftly. Otherwise, he'll be here in this hall with a sword to our necks. Do none of you understand that?"

"We understand the possibility of it," one of the men said. "But where is the proof of it?"

Unferth shook his head, dismayed. "Horta has told you it is so. What more do you need?"

"Horta has said that Brand won a victory. He has said the army we sent is defeated. He has said much, but I will believe it better when word returns with one of our own men. As yet, we have heard nothing."

There it was. Unferth knew he was losing control, and he must act decisively to regain it. Not long ago, his very word was law. Now, though he knew Horta would be proved right in what he claimed, the men awaited their own proof. The irony was that the military loss they yet did not believe was the thing that emboldened them.

Horta adjusted the bearskin serape that hung over his shoulders. If he was offended, he gave no sign. But he never did.

"Brand won a great victory," the magician assured them. "Of that, you can be certain. I would tell you how I know, but it would burn your souls to ash. Believe, and you have an opportunity to act quickly and turn adversity into triumph. Delay, and the kingdom will slip through your fingers."

"Easy for you to say," said another warrior at the table. "But why should we believe you?"

Unferth ground his teeth. He knew Horta's powers. He knew something of the magic the man possessed. Very likely, it *would* burn the souls of most men to ash.

A look passed between them. Horta's gaze said that magic was his province, and controlling the Callenor was Unferth's. The magician's disciple, Olbata, sat beside his master and stared at the men around the table, his eyes dark with hidden thoughts.

Once more Unferth slammed his hand down on the table, and this time he shouted with it.

"Fools!" He looked around, turning his cold gaze on the counselors. It was the gaze of a man who had killed, the gaze of a man who might yet hold the power of life and death over them. And their mood for defiance washed away, at least for the moment.

But he did not have a chance to speak. The fire in the pit at the center of the hall flickered and smoked. The air grew suddenly chill, and an acrid odor filled it.

Unferth looked at Horta, thinking he had begun to work magic. But there was dread in the other man's eyes. It was the first time he had ever seen Horta display fear. He had always thought the man possessed a heart of stone.

Horta stood and moved to the back of the room, drawing Unferth with him. Unferth did not resist.

All around the table men seemed confused. Some drew their swords. A sudden wind roared to life, and within it came another sound, regular and forceful like the beating of vast wings.

Unferth pressed his back against the wall. Even as he did so the wind died away and the great door to the hall crashed open with a booming clatter of oak planks and hinges. Timbers rattled, the hall itself shook, and within the opening a thing of huge shadows hulked. There it stood a moment, surveying those in the room. Its head swiveled, and Unferth thought that it sniffed at the air.

Horta, his own back to the wall, moved. Briefly Unferth glimpsed the man withdraw a leaf from one of his many pouches with trembling hands and slip it into his mouth. Then the man whispered in his ear. "Do not move nor speak, no matter what happens, and all will be well."

The mass of shadows in the doorway began to move. The intruder walked like a man, though it limped. Ten feet high it stood, at least, and as it came into the room the fire in the pit flared to life with a crackle of popping wood and colored smoke.

With the leaping flames came greater light, and Unferth saw the thing clearly. It had wings, vast and bulky that were furled behind it and still part-hidden by shadow. It had the form of a man, but its head was that of a bat.

"Shemfal," whispered Horta beside him. Unferth did not know who or what this creature was, but the name slipped into his mind like a dagger of fear.

On the creature came, striding like a king. Yet the limp marred his presence, and Unferth wondered what power walked the world that could give injury to such as this.

One of the warriors at the table screamed a battle-cry and leapt at the thing. His bright sword flashed through the air, but Shemfal, barely seeming to move, brushed the blade aside with his arm and then smote the man a hammer-like blow.

The warrior fell dead. Others had drawn their swords, but they milled about in fear and did not attack. They saw no way to defeat such a creature, and neither did Unferth. But he must trust in Horta. The magician had said all would be well.

Shemfal came to a stop. His dark eyes, round and burning with a fierce gaze beneath pointed ears, turned to Horta.

"The price must be paid, mortal."

"Indeed, great lord."

Horta said no more, but his glance turned to Olbata. So also the gaze of Shemfal.

The massive wings of the creature unfurled slightly, and he pointed with a bony hand, black talons dripping from the ends of his fingers like curved daggers.

"You are mine, mortal. Come hither."

Olbata trembled. He swung to Horta, his mouth working several times before words were voiced.

"Why? Did I not serve you well?"

Horta turned a cool gaze upon him. "Yes, you did. Yet also, you knew the risks. Knowledge does not come without cost. You are unlucky to pay the price, for it was no fault of your own. But the risk was always there. Do not dishonor yourself by trying to fight your fate. It is written now."

"It is written in my blood!"

Horta did not answer, merely looking at his pupil as though at an ant beneath his feet.

Unferth admired him in that moment. He was so calm, so assured of the rightness of his actions. Whatever lay behind this, no one understood fully but Horta. And yet Unferth guessed that this creature had been summoned from the pit and constrained to perform an errand. Now, it sought payment for the deed done. Such was the way of demons, which this thing must surely be.

Olbata swung back to the creature and swiftly began to chant. He raised his hand, a tiny statuette in his fingers, and this he held high as some sort of talisman.

Shemfal laughed. His wings beat and he darted forward, one hand snaking out to grab his victim by the throat.

Olbata screamed, but the sound was muffled. With another beat of wings Shemfal hovered in the air a moment, and then he glided toward the fire pit.

The flames roared once more as though in greeting. The demon descended, Olbata thrashing as tongues of fire licked his flesh. And then the fire pit was no more. In its place opened a fissure in the earth, and down in its depths Unferth glimpsed a mighty cavern, lit by flickering flames and wreathed in shadows. A dark throne rose in the center, and all manner of wicked things moved and writhed about it.

Fire flared once more, and Olbata's screams died away in a puff of greasy smoke. When that cleared, the vision of the underworld was gone and the fire pit burned as it always had. Silence filled the hall, but the beating of Unferth's heart thundered in his chest.

Here though was an opportunity to assert control again, and he took it. Despite his terror, he wore a guise of nonchalance.

He stepped forward with confidence and ease. Righting a chair that had been spilled when the men rose from the table and drew their swords, he sat down and leaned back comfortably.

"Our meeting is not yet over," he said. "Come, sit down. We must continue."

The men returned to the table. One by one, reluctantly, blades were sheathed.

"See," Unferth said. "Horta is a magician of power. If he tells us Brand beat the army we sent, it is so. Do not doubt it."

One of the warriors scraped his chair loudly as he sat. "If Horta is a magician of such power, how is it that Brand still lives?"

Unferth felt his frustration rise again. This time it was intensified by his terror at what had just happened, and he wanted to reach out and throttle the man questioning him. Was he not a king? Was it right that they contended with his every word?

Horta was the one who answered the man though, his voice smooth and measured.

"That will be remedied," the magician said. "Twice now I have tried to kill Brand, and he has survived. The man's life is charmed. But his luck must run out soon."

"How will you do it?" Unferth asked.

Horta shrugged. "I have … ways. Best that you do not know them, for they would only serve to give you nightmares."

Unferth believed him. He had no real desire to know the details. Almost, he could feel sorry for Brand.

The magician's gaze showed nothing, but there was a hint of amusement to the curl of his lips. He knew exactly what Unferth was thinking.

"This much I will say," Horta continued, now addressing all of the men at the table. "I will look after Brand, but whether I kill him or not there is yet his army to defeat. It will not disperse now, even at his death. That is a problem you must deal with."

It was sound advice, and Unferth knew it. The Duthenor were raised against him now, and everything he had striven for could be lost. He would not let that happen.

"Horta has summed up the situation well," he said. "We must defeat Brand's army, but how best shall we do that?"

The men seemed sullen, and most kept glancing at the fire pit. Horta excused himself and walked away. Unferth watched him go, knowing that he would gather his disciples and initiate some dreadful rite of magic. What its nature would be, Unferth did not even want to contemplate. But he had a feeling that the little magician took Brand's survival as a personal insult now. Brand, at least, would be one less problem soon.

"Well?" he said to the men. "How shall we defeat the enemy? Shall we march against them, or let them come here and spend themselves against our defenses?"

2. The Blood of a Hero

It was the morning after the battle. It was the dawn of a new day, after a great victory. And yet Brand found little joy in his triumph. Others had paid for it with their blood.

Haldring was especially on his mind as the army readied to march. He had instructed Sighern to hold the Dragon Banner of the Duthenor high, and it hung limply in the still air from the long staff it was attached to. Some had wanted to throw it away, soiled by Haldring's blood as it was, and make a new one. He would have none of that. The blood of a hero was a better emblem than a dragon.

But even in death he used her, as he had in life. At least, he could not help feeling so. He had not known what would happen, but he had guessed. And he had set the example himself. He had touched the cloth first thing in the morning, head bowed, and whispered an oath. *I will try to show the courage you did, and fight until my last breath even as you. Nothing shall stop me.*

Many had seen him. Some had heard his words. And when he had walked away, a line of soldiers followed his lead. They touched the cloth and said the words. It would bind them, fill them with purpose, and give morale to the army. Already word was spreading through the ranks. A legend was growing, and by the end of the day every soldier would have done the same thing, become part of the same group. In years to come, if they lived, they would tell their children and their grandchildren that they had sworn Haldring's oath.

Brand took the reins of his horse and looked ahead with steely eyes. How had he come to this? What cruel fate had shaped him so? He could not do anything, even grieve the death of a friend, without turning it into a means of manipulating soldiers and strengthening the army. And yet, if he did not, the army would be weaker and more likely to lose. Then, all those who had died, Haldring included, would have perished in vain. What he was doing was wrong, but it was also right, and he yearned for a simpler world. But he knew he would never have it.

"March!" he called.

Nearby, a man blew a horn and the army began to move. It would be no swift march, not today. Few were unscathed by yesterday's battle, one way or another. Including himself. And the army was smaller than it was. Behind them they left the dead. The wounded had already been moved to villages close to hand.

The sun rose to his left, for the army was heading south. He had a goal, but as yet no destination. That goal was the overthrow of Unferth. The man was at the heart of his woes, ever since childhood. He had murdered his parents. Who knew how many of the Duthenor had been killed at his hands? And last, though it was not murder, he was the ultimate cause of Haldring's death. For all those things he would pay.

Brand remained silent as the army progressed along the High Way. His thoughts kept him occupied, dark as they were. Even young Sighern, walking close by his side, recognized his mood and did not disturb it. Shorty and Taingern, leading their own horses on his other side, had long years ago learned when to leave him to himself.

A dark mood such as this came on him seldom, and anger and frustration less often still, but they had him now in a grip of iron.

The miles passed, and the rhythm of walking occupied his body but freed his mind. Walking was a good way to think, but it was calming too, and his mood gradually softened. He must put aside anger and vengeance. They were useless emotions. At least, they were not good in the long term. And that was how he must think. His every deed and action must be for the benefit and future of the army and the Duthgar. His purpose was to free them of Unferth, and that goal, and that goal alone, must guide his tactics. His personal feelings must be put aside.

He called the first halt of the day. The soldiers wasted no time sitting or lying down. They were wise now in the ways of war, and rested whenever opportunity arose.

Brand saw Taingern glance at him, assessing his mood. The man always read him well, and he must have sensed the change in his temper, for he spoke.

"We're making fair time," he said, "despite everyone's weariness."

"Fair time," Shorty echoed, "but to where? We're heading south, but does that mean we're striking for Unferth himself?"

Brand sat down, and the others joined him. Sighern did likewise, but he still gripped the staff that held up the banner.

"A good question," Brand answered. "Whatever we do next, our direction must be southward. But we still have a choice. Gather more men as we go, or seek to strike swiftly while the enemy is chagrined by their loss."

Taingern seemed relieved. "So you have not decided yet?"

"No."

"That's good. A hasty decision often leads to trouble."

"Wise words," Brand said with a grin, "but what you mean is that a decision based on emotion hinders sound judgement."

13

Taingern looked thoughtful. "No one would blame you for being emotional."

"Possibly not. But the Duthgar needs more from me than that. What I must decide now is how best to defeat Unferth."

Shorty grinned. "Strike out for him now, so that our army follows hot on the heels of the news of his loss. Catch him with his pants down, so to speak."

"Not quite the imagery I wanted," Brand laughed. "But your point is well made. And what of you, Taingern? What do you advise?"

Taingern stretched out on the ground and plucked a stem of grass, which he then rolled between his fingers.

"These are the two questions we need to consider. How many men can Unferth still muster? And how many more can you gather to you as you go? No doubt, the slower you travel the more you will get."

"I cannot be sure of exact numbers," Brand answered. "But likely enough, Unferth could muster another five thousand men."

"Fewer though, the quicker you strike for him and the less chance he has to prepare," Shorty suggested.

"Quite right," Brand agreed. "But our own army is now down to a little under a thousand men after yesterday's battle. If I march quickly, I may only have time to double that. I could end up facing Unferth with an army of two thousand, but even caught by surprise he might be able to match that."

"And if you march more slowly," Taingern said, "how many more men could you gather?"

Brand thought on that. "Another two thousand, I would think. That would give me an army of four thousand in total."

"It seems to me," Shorty said, "that the slower you go the more you will end up being outnumbered."

"So it could prove," Brand said. "But there's one other thing to consider."

Shorty grunted. "You're right. The magician."

"Exactly. What he's capable of in a battle, we don't know. But his magic is powerful, so we can be sure to expect something. And there's one more thing."

"What's that?"

"Horta may learn of our victory last night by sorcerous means. Unferth may have warning, and therefore a chance to prepare long before normal messages reach him."

Shorty kicked at the ground with his heel. "That puts a different light on things."

Brand remained calm. Even after such a great victory, all was still in doubt. His instincts were the same as Shorty's though. Move quickly and try to use speed itself as a weapon. But Unferth could at this very moment be thinking the same.

It was an interesting line of thought. Would Unferth come to him and attack? It was not really in the man's nature. He preferred to move in the shadows and manipulate things like a spider in his web. And yet, he had been poked. How would he react?

The more he considered it the more he formed a definite belief. Unferth would have word of the battle swiftly. Horta would see to that. When news reached the rest of them, support for Unferth would diminish. He would begin to lose control. He would worry that other uprisings among the Duthenor would occur, separate from what was happening here. How best to counterattack that? By moving swiftly himself and attacking. And he would do so with everything he had to try to crush the rebellion definitively.

"Gentlemen," Brand said. "I think we'll meet Unferth on the road, for he'll be coming to us."

"Likely enough," Taingern agreed. "And once more his forces will outnumber ours."

"Indeed. And he will think to have the advantage of surprise. But surprise works two ways."

Shorty grinned at him. "I like it when you have a plan. And I'm pretty sure I can see the glint of one in your eye right now. Am I right?"

3. Battle and Victory!

To march forward and fight, or to establish a fortified position were the choices Unferth gave his advisers. No one suggested any alternatives.

"Let Brand come," said several of the men. "We can excavate earth ramparts. No matter the size of his army, we'll have the advantage then."

"And what if he skirts our fortified position and takes the king's hall?" others argued. "Then the Duthenor will rise against us to a man and nothing will stop them."

Another group were all for defending the hall itself. "What need have we for ramparts? Our army will outnumber his. All we need is to hold our ground until he comes and then defeat him."

Few were the voices that argued in favor of marching forth to attack Brand. But to these Unferth paid most attention. It was the way he leaned himself. Too much was happening, and he had too little control of it. Setting out on a march would bring the men together, give him a greater position of authority as leader and help fortify his standing as a king. When Brand was beaten, there would be no dissent to his rule then. That was the one thing he must do above all others, and as quickly as possible.

His nephew had been the foremost proponent of this strategy. "Attack him!" Gormengil pressed. "Why should we suffer such as Brand to raise arms against us in our own realm? We have the advantage of surprise, thanks to Horta. Let us use that, and blot him and those who support him from the history of the Duthgar. Better that

17

than to debate and whine and worry like a pack of half-witted dogs!"

Gormengil had not held back. It was his way, and he had enemies for it. But he had supporters too, and many of them. He was one to watch. Unferth had named him as heir, for he had no son of his own, but he intended to live a long while yet. But Gormengil knew no restraint when it came to ambition. What he said now was right, but he was to be trusted less for it. He always had secret motives.

"I have listened and considered and weighed all of your views," Unferth said. "This is my decision. Gather the army. We march to war, and we march at dawn tomorrow."

He turned to his personal servant. "Fetch my axe and armor. I ride to battle and victory!"

The man hurried off. He would retrieve the sacred battle apparel of the chieftains of the Callenor, what had never been worn in the lands of the Duthenor. Unferth had taken the rule without bloodshed, but there would be bloodshed now. The Duthgar would swim in a sea of red, and Brand would sink beneath the crimson tide.

Swiftly he gave orders and made plans. And the more he took charge the better the men obeyed him. It was a lesson learned, and he would not soon forget it. A leader must impose his will, and the more he did that the less dissention there would be.

As he slept that night though, the whisper of doubt returned to him. What if Brand won again, despite still having the smaller army? What if Horta failed once more to kill him by sorcery? And most of all, threaded through all his lesser fears was the greatest of them, the one that he did not just worry over but had seen begin, the loss of his authority over those he ruled. It was slipping away, and though he had drawn tight the reins of leadership once more, the dissention would return quickly at any setback.

It was a long night, and Unferth tossed and turned and drifted finally into a dark sleep. And he dreamed as he had never dreamed before. Here, in the shadow-world of his thought, he found his true self and the strength that was inside him.

A white-coated bull charged him, dark eyes blazing and head tilted down, his horns set to rip and impale. But with a deft touch of Unferth's hand the beast's anger was stayed. It shook its head and then wandered off, grazing the sparse grass nearby as though nothing had happened.

Unferth strode away. A hawk flashed through the air, all wings and speed and confidence. That was him now. Unferth the hawk, lord of the sky.

The ground beneath his boots was withered and dry. Dead grass crunched beneath his tread. The sun beat down, but even as he felt the oppression of it, he thought of a cooling breeze and one rose to caress his skin.

Ahead was a range of mountains, purple-blue in the heat haze. There he knew he would find good shade beneath stunted trees or in the lee of some cliff. He turned toward it.

In the way of dreams he found himself there straightaway, winding his way down a rocky slope. There were no trees, stunted or otherwise, and he felt a prickle of unease as though unseen eyes watched him. What land was this that he dreamed of? It was not like the green hills of his home.

The heat dissipated. Steep walls of stone now towered either side over his path, and he walked down a canyon that was silent, still and peaceful. It was daylight, though dim in the declivity, and the stars filled the daytime sky like a thousand beautiful lights.

Benevolence washed over him in waves, and all was right with the world. A clatter of hooves sounded ahead, and some sort of animal like a mountain sheep leapt nimbly away from a pool of water and disappeared into vague shadows on the canyon sides. Unferth moved toward the pool.

It was clear as glass, but on its dark surface he saw the reflection of his own face. It seemed to him that he was a king of old. Wisdom etched his features, but there was strength there too. The courage of the heroes of legend was in his glance, and upon his head sat a crown of stars.

He knelt and drank of the water, finding it sweet and intoxicating as wine. It refreshed him, cured his thirst and filled him with strength.

With a graceful movement he stood, and found that he was not alone. A young man, dressed in strange robes of a golden hue, sat cross-legged on the stone shelf beside the pool.

"Greetings," the man said. "I trust the water was pleasant?"

"Indeed."

The young man gestured, and Unferth knew it as an invitation to join him. He too sat cross-legged, opposite his companion.

"My name is Char-harash."

Unferth inclined his head. The man before him was highborn, probably royalty, that much was evident, but he himself was a king. He bowed to no one, though even seated he had the feeling that he should. He dismissed it.

Char-harash smiled, his face open and honest. "A king of your standing ever seeks wise counselors, does he not? And yet the voices of the multitude always clamor in your ears with petty concerns. Tell me that it is so?"

Unferth was pleased. Here was a man who understood his situation. "It is so."

The young man nodded sagely. "It is always thus. But you are special. To you, I offer my services. The wisdom of the ages is at your disposal, and I shall aid you in your troubles. This is what you wish, above all else, yes?"

Unferth bowed his head. "You read my mind."

The other man gazed calmly at him. "If I am to help you, you must say yes."

"Yes, my lord. I wish your help above all else."

Char-harash smiled. It was an easy smile, a smile to instill confidence. On another man, it would have seemed cruel. But on a lord such as Char-harash, it was fitting.

"Tell me of Brand."

"He is the rightful lord of the Duthenor," Unferth said. A vague feeling of unease overtook him once more, but the young man reached out and touched his hand.

"All is well. There shall only be the truth between us. That will be good, will it not?"

"Yes, my lord."

"What sort of man is Brand?"

"He is dangerous and hard to kill. His skill with a sword is said to be sublime. And he possesses magic too."

The younger man considered that. "But you could beat him, could you not?"

"Of course."

"What is his weakness?"

Unferth wanted to answer quickly, but this required thought. The water in the pool remained still and clear, and the gaze of the young man was intent.

"He has the weakness of all good men. Morals constrain him. If he cast them away, he could be truly great."

The young man did not seem best pleased at that answer. Unferth sensed he wanted to know more about Brand's personality, his style of leadership and the type of military strategies he employed. But Unferth knew none of those things.

Char-harash looked at him solemnly. "And how do you intend to beat Brand?"

"I will crush him by weight of numbers and surprise."

The young man considered that. "Yes, these are strong tools in the hand of a skilled warlord. Strong indeed, but the warlord who wields them must be the best." The young man looked at him intently once more. "Are you the best, Unferth?"

"I am. I was a chieftain, but I made myself a king. I united two tribes and I—"

"Who is second best to you?"

It was an easy question and Unferth answered quickly. "Gormengil, my lord."

"Tell me about him."

"The blood of chieftains is in his veins. He is young, ruthless and ambitious. He is quick to find trouble, but he can be subtle too, especially so for one of his age, though it's not normally his way. And he can fight also. He's a great warrior, greater than myself. Most people say he is the best fighter among the Callenor."

Char-harash remained quiet, listening carefully, and then he seemed to come to a decision. He raised his hand and Unferth stopped speaking.

"All will be well," the young lord said. "Rest easy and sleep now. Brand is a grave threat, but already steps have been taken against him and he is snared in a trap."

"But what shall I—"

"Hush," Char-harash commanded. "Sleep. All will be well."

The young lord reached out and brushed his fingers against Unferth's brow. A wave of contentment rolled over him. Sleepiness came with it and he felt his mind drift. The little canyon grew darker. The pool was lost from sight. Only Char-harash remained, a golden-clad lord standing tall and proud as a king of old. For the first time, Unferth saw that in his left hand was a wooden rod, pale white and gleaming with a sheen of sorcerous power. In his right was a sword, the edge wickedly sharp.

Char-harash leveled the wooden rod at him. "Sleep," he commanded. And Unferth slept.

The night wore on, and Unferth dreamed once more, but he did not meet again the golden-robed lord who promised to help him. When he woke, he felt better rested than he had in years. And calm too, considering that he marched to war.

He put the night's dreams from his mind. Reality called instead, for today would be a day of history, for he himself would ride to war and the armor and weapon of his great ancestor that founded the Callenor realm would once more inspire terror among their foes.

His manservant entered the room, bearing a tray of food. He did not speak, having long since learned to answer questions only. Unferth wished he had more like him: well trained, silent and obedient.

He quickly ate a meal of bread, thickly sliced ham and soft cheese. While he did so, the manservant waited nearby should he want something. But all Unferth wanted to do was ride. He dismissed him, finished eating and then looked at the armor. It was laid out on a chest before him, and it sent a thrill up his spine.

Reverently, he pulled the mail-shirt over his head, placed the gauntlets on his hand and the helm on his head. Then he took up the weapon of his forefathers. It felt good in his hand. Taking a deep breath, he flung open the door and strode down the length of the hall and outside.

Warriors gazed at him, and then bowed. There was fear in their eyes, or so he thought. If not, there should be. He knew he looked the part of a battle king. And soon the Duthenor would see him, and tremble at the folly of even thinking about rebellion.

He led a procession of his closest friends and best warriors down out of the hall and into the field beyond the village. Here his army was gathered, or at least the first part of it.

Over a thousand men waited. Others would swell the army in the next village and the next. But it was these men who saw him first, and their eyes were riveted to him. This was a sight most had not seen in their lifetime.

Unferth came to a standstill near where his mount was tethered. He stood before it so all could see him. The chain mail shirt he wore was of the finest steel, each ring wrought and linked by cunning skill beyond the reach of mortal blacksmiths. It was lighter than it should be, stronger than it seemed, invincible to blade or dart. The dwarves of the Anast Dennath mountains had made it, and spells were woven into the metal at both forging and joining. So at least the legends claimed. But what drew the eye was that each link was lacquered red, crimson as bright blood, and no amount of time nor strike by any enemy had ever tarnished it.

Upon his head rested a mighty helm. This also was fashioned by the dwarves, and spells were upon it too. Engraved into the same red-lacquered metal was a single rune: karak, which meant victory in their tongue. From the eye slit Unferth gazed out and saw his army. Pride and strength filled him.

He raised high now in a sudden thrust the weapon of his forefathers. It was made of the same metal as the rest, though lacquered black rather than red. The weight was somewhat less than it should be, for it was a double-bladed axe. Each half swept back like wings, but there was a stabbing spike in the center, slightly curved like a beak so that it could also hook and gouge. This was a weapon of legend to the Callenor, for it was made for their founding chieftain. And it was made in the image of the symbol he took as his own: a raven.

Unferth gave the axe a flourish, and then he slipped the haft through a leather thong on his horse's saddle and mounted.

The men began to chant. *The Crimson Lord! The Crimson Lord! The Crimson Lord!*

He liked it. Once more he felt confidence and invincibility flood through his veins. He would destroy Brand. And yet even as he thought of his enemy the whisper of doubt returned. He knew it would always be there. The only way to silence it would be to kill his opponent.

He kicked his horse forward and the army began to move with him, still chanting.

4. The Trickster

Horta was pleased. The place he had chosen was fitting for his purpose. And it would need to be, for the summoning of a god was no task to carry out unless all was in order.

Idly, he slipped a norhanu leaf into his mouth and sucked upon it. Too often he did so now, for useful as the herb was it also was a poison. But these were dangerous days. To survive them, he must take risks that otherwise he would not dare.

The hilltop was perfect. He hated this green land, swept often by wind and rain and trailing mists. But from here, he could see all around for miles. The air was sweet and pure, and it carried the scent of grass and herb and flower. Birds wheeled to and fro, and on a lower ridge he had glimpsed a herd of deer. Down below the halls and villages of men were so distant as to nearly not be there at all. That was good, very good indeed.

"Is all well, master?"

Horta did not turn to look. He did not like the Arnhaten to speak with him at times like this. Yet, now that Olbata was gone, he must look to another of his disciples for a chief helper.

After a while, he glanced at the other man. It was Tanata. He was a quiet person, secretive and sly. He had the makings of a magician, although he seemed very young for the dark arts that must be learned.

Horta sighed. "All is well, Tanata." He may as well begin to teach the lad what he knew.

"Then why do you look sad?"

Horta looked out once more at the view. "Because it is not easy to be a magician. Oh, to be sure, the spells and rituals are easy enough. Anyone can learn them and carry them out."

"Then what *is* hard?"

"Doing what must be done is hard, even when you know it must."

"It does not sound hard, master."

"And yet it is. Perhaps you need to be an old man to know that."

Tanata did not reply to that, and Horta shivered in the silence. He had a sense that one day, years from now, a young man would ask Tanata the same question. He wondered if his disciple would give a better answer.

Horta brushed the pensive mood from his mind. It was not like him, and it would only hinder what he had to do.

"See!" he said, rousing himself and sweeping out a long arm. "All about us is nature. The hand of man is distant. How will this help us in what we intend?"

Tanata did not answer straightaway. He considered the question, and Horta felt his mood lighten. Here was one who might have the temper to learn the mysteries.

"We seek to summon a god," Tanata answered at length. "And the gods are connected to the land, born from it even. There is power in the land. It lives, and its life will aid us."

Horta was surprised. It was a good answer. "And why avoid proximity to the works of men?"

"Because human life is fleeting. Human minds are filled with emotions that roil and seethe and disrupt the peace of nature. The land is the great power, and it is to this we must connect to perform our rites."

Horta turned his gaze full upon the young man. "And you? Do you feel the power of the land?"

Tanata gave a slight nod. "When I close my eyes, I feel it. When I am alone, I feel it."

"And now?"

"I feel nothing at the moment."

It was another good answer. Many others would have lied.

"Do not concern yourself with that. Your senses will strengthen over time. It is enough to know the theory. Practice will make your senses keener as the years pass. And you have many long years of study ahead of you."

The young man bowed, but remained silent and gave no foolish response. Horta was growing to like him.

He walked toward the flat patch of ground near the very top of the hill where the Arnhaten were gathered. What the boy had said about the land was true, but it was especially true just now. The god he intended to summon was Su-sarat. She was an old god, strongly connected to the land. She was the serpent god, the Trickster, and her symbol was the puff adder. The ancients had named her well, for she was tricksome as her namesake that flicked its tongue or tail to attract prey and then struck with killing venom. Tricksome indeed, but she was the one needed when other, and more direct, methods had failed.

He approached the spring that bubbled up water from the patch of ground he had chosen for the ceremony. There would be no fire here. The gods had their preferences, and Su-sarat would like the winding trail of water that turned and twisted its way down the hill. Serpentine it was, and more than many of the gods she had a greater affinity for the animalistic form she took.

"Gather round," Horta commanded the Arnhaten.

They came to him, but he saw doubtful looks on some of their faces. The fate of Olbata had bred discontent. So too had Brand's continuing survival. It eroded faith in the power of the gods. But they would see. A mortal might defy divinity for a time, but not for long.

"The sacred words of the summoning chant are the same," Horta told them. "But we will not stand or walk. Instead, we will sit in a line, a sinuous line like a snake. And I will be at its head, facing you."

He gestured and Tanata took the lead position of the line facing him. Some of the others did not like this. They knew it for a sign of favor, and much as they did not like how things had turned out lately, they still lusted after knowledge of the mysteries. Tanata would have to be careful, otherwise one of them might kill him if a secret opportunity arose. It had been the same for Olbata. They did not mourn his passing, only the manner of it. The same could have been done to them.

Slowly, he began to chant. His words were not the same as the Arnhaten. They joined him, voicing the sacred rite, but his words were the ones of greater power. His words were the ones lifted into the heavens and shot like an arrow from a bow toward a target. Yet the Arnhaten were the bow, for by their power they sped his arrow.

"Hear me, O Mistress of the Sands. Hear my call, Dancer in the Night. Thy servant needs you. Come to me, Queen of Secrets, I beseech thee!"

The water issuing from the spring frothed and bubbled, and it surged down the slope of the hill with a hiss of steam. A sulfurous odor wafted into the air, and the earth began to tremble. Even seated, the chanting Arnhaten swayed, the line of them like a serpent themselves.

Horta continued. Once begun, the Rite of Summoning must always be finished, else it was considered an insult to the god. He was not so foolish as to risk that.

He lifted his voice higher, his words rising and falling, turning and twisting through the air with the thrum of his own power. He knew what would happen next, for he once had been an Arnhaten and sat in a line as did these. He knew what would happen, and yet it shocked him still.

The column of disciples began to transform. An image lay over them, vague and faint, of a massive serpent. As the chanting continued, the image grew stronger, and soon it was an image no more.

Su-sarat lay before him, her dark serpentine body coiling and sliding over the grass. Yet her head was perfectly still, the slit-like orbs of her eyes fixed upon him and her pink tongue probing the air for his scent.

She raised herself, showing the bright yellow of her belly. From there she could strike, and that would be death, but Horta had long since schooled himself to such risks.

Slowly, he bowed his head. "O mighty Su-sarat, the earth is graced by your form. I am humbled by your beauty."

Thus had the words of greeting been handed down to him. It was not his place to dispute them, but rather to uphold custom.

The goddess towered above him, her head serpentine, and yet there was something human in it also.

"Why dost thou thus? You call upon me, yet only when my brothers have failed thee."

"O great one," Horta answered. "Brute force has not availed me, and so I call upon you, last but not least. Yours is the strength I need, for it is built on wisdom and understanding and knowledge of the frailties of men."

Su-sarat licked the air, and tension hung between them.

"Great goddess," Horta continued, cold sweat beading on the skin of his face. "You are a trickster, a mistress of deceit and a veiler of the truth. Yours is the power I need, for you can succeed where others have failed."

Her shadow fell over him. "Do you disparage my brothers?"

"Nay, Lady. I speak only the truth. The fault is mine, for I did not explain how dangerous my enemy is."

The sky seemed to dim, and he felt the cold breath of her mouth upon his face. Then followed the wet flick of her tongue against his fever-hot skin.

"I taste your fear."

Horta did not know what she meant. Fear of Brand? Fear of death? Fear of failing to carry out his great task? All could be true.

"O great one, I live to serve. If I have displeased you, strike me down. If you take mercy upon me, I beseech you, aid me in my task as only you can."

Silence fell. She made no answer. Sweat dripped from Horta's brow, but he dared not move to wipe it away.

"Tell me of Brand," Su-sarat commanded. "He intrigues me."

Horta tried not to show any relief. It was best when dealing with gods to be humble and yet confident. Flattery was wise, also.

"Brand is just a man. And yet, in some manner, he is touched by fate. He is a skilled warrior, and he possesses the use of magic. Without these things, and luck, he would not have defeated the emissaries of your brothers."

Su-sarat swayed in the air, at least her upper body and head. The rest of her coiled restlessly over the grass.

"And why is Brand, as you say, touched by fate?"

"I do not know, mistress. But that he is, I am sure."

"Perhaps you say this merely because he thwarts you?"

"The man *does* thwart me, and this happens so seldom that, truly, he must be touched by fate to do so."

"Ah, Horta. I remember you. I know you. I have watched your rise among magicians. You are too soft, and a streak of kindness runs through you. Yes, Brand is touched by fate. He has a destiny. Yet still, had you but tried hard enough, you could have killed him. You needed no aid from gods for this. Had you convinced Unferth to send a greater army your enemy would now be lying dead on a battlefield."

Horta felt a swell of pride. The goddess had noted him, and watched. Yet pride was an empty emotion, useless for the most part and dangerous beside.

"You are correct, for your wisdom is as great as your beauty. I had thought Unferth under my control, but that was prideful of me. He still rules the Duthgar, unwisely, and I did not assert my wishes upon him. Brand is just a man, though an accomplished one, and he should have died by sword long since. I am rebuked."

Su-sarat hissed, and the noise of it filled the air. Horta realized it was her laughter.

"Do not fear, Horta. You have failed in this, yet still do you serve the gods well. For this, and because Brand intrigues me, I will help you."

Horta bowed his head. "And the price, mistress?" It was a fool who never agreed on the price with a god first. Afterwards, it was too late.

"The usual price is blood, Horta."

So it was. And he would do what he must, but it was too soon to lose Tanata. He had been near invisible before, but after Olbata had had been taken, the man had proved to be everywhere at just the right time. It was no coincidence either that he had not drawn attention to himself until now. Olbata or one of the others may have killed him. He was patient as well as useful. The man could go far, if he lived.

Su-sarat moved above him, her yellow belly glistening before him. The movement sent her coils roiling, and the tip of her tale rattled like the puff adder of his faraway home.

"The usual price is blood," the goddess repeated. "A death for a death. And yet, truly, this Brand intrigues me greatly. I will not kill him, but have him for a slave instead. I would hear the words of flattery that you use, but voiced from his mouth. Would this displease you, Horta?"

It was not usual for one of the gods to talk thus to a man, even a great magician. But Su-sarat was capricious. She obeyed no rules save her own, followed no guide except her own cold heart. Horta wished Brand dead, and yet, bent to her will and in her service, he would be a threat no more.

"It would not displease me, O Mistress of the Sands. And for your service, what price do you set?" He had not forgotten, nor would ever fail to set the price before the bargain was made. The lore of magicians was clear on that point, and the story of the one magician who had failed to do so a matter of legend.

"This is my price, Horta." Her figure loomed over him, and then she bent her head forward until the cold breath of her mouth was upon his ear, and the whisper of her voice filled his mind.

5. A Place of Ill Omen

Brand looked solemn, but there was a glint in his eye. "I have a plan, but it won't be liked. Not one bit, but it *will* serve us well."

Taingern gave a faint shrug. "The worst plans are often liked best, and the best the least. Until the day of reckoning, at any rate."

Brand knew the truth of those words. Taingern, as ever, was philosophical. But he understood better than most the hearts of people. He would know also that once a disliked plan proved successful, everyone would claim to have supported it. Such was life.

"Well then," Shorty said. "What do you have in mind?"

"Unferth is likely to attack us, thinking that his best option. And it is. Therefore, we must do the opposite of what he expects."

"He expects us to march toward him, and a battle at some point, wherever our forces draw close."

"Exactly," Brand agreed. "So I'll deny him that."

Shorty scratched his head. "How? Will you try to play cat and mouse with him as you've done so far, building your army as you move into unexpected places?"

"I could try that, but the larger my army the harder that becomes. Sooner or later, he'll corner me and force a battle with superior numbers."

"Then how will you deny him what he wants?"

"All I need is a fortress. Men can gather to me there just as easily as on the road. My army can grow, and when the battle comes the advantage of his greater numbers will be lost attacking a fortified defense."

Sighern spoke for the first time. "But there *are* no fortified defenses in the Duthgar. We don't build fortresses."

Shorty glanced at him. "Brand has told me the same thing, more than once." He crossed his arms. "But if he says it, it must be true."

"I have said," Brand agreed, "that the Duthenor don't build fortresses, nor do we have skill at attacking or defending them. But that doesn't mean that no fortresses have ever been built in the Duthgar."

Sighern's face paled. "You can't be serious!"

"Deadly serious. It's the advantage we need. And if you're surprised, then Unferth likely will be too. He'll not even consider the possibility, I'll warrant."

"Out with it, Brand." Shorty asked. "What's the surprise?"

"The fortress I'm speaking of is called Pennling Palace. It's an ancient place, as old as the Duthgar and part of its legends, but probably older by far than that."

"If nothing else," Shorty said, "at least it has a fair-sounding name. I've been in many fortresses, but none so far would pass for a palace."

Sighern looked bleak. "Don't be fooled by the name. Although Pennling is a great hero, this place has a reputation of ill omen."

Brand glanced back at the army. They were growing restless, for the rest break had been longer than usual.

"Yes, it's a place of ill omen," Brand agreed. "And the men will not like it at all."

"Why does it have such a bad reputation?" Taingern asked.

"A good question," Brand replied. "But the answer will have to wait. It's time to march again, but first I must tell this decision to the men."

They stood up and walked the short distance to the front ranks. The army stood in response, thinking they were about to march again, but Brand addressed them instead.

"Men," he said loudly, though it was short of a yell. "I have made a decision, and I'll tell it to you now. I hide nothing from you, whether good or ill. And you will consider this ill, but I ask that you have trust in me. Have I not led you well so far? And likewise, this will work out for the best in the end."

Brand stopped speaking. He waited for his words to be passed back to the men furthest away.

"Where do we go now?" a man in the front row asked. "For that surely is the decision you reached."

"Where do we go?" Brand repeated. "Where else, but to the place we must. I believe Unferth will march to war himself. He'll outnumber us. Of this, we should have little fear. Already we have beaten a greater force, and we can do so again. But where I take you now, the place will lessen his advantage."

"And where's that?" It was Hruidgar who spoke, the huntsman who had led them through the swamp. There was a look in his eye too; he was a well-traveled man. Brand had the feeling he had guessed their destination.

"Pennling Palace," Brand answered. "That's the place for us."

The men reacted as he had thought. Many were the dark looks and the muttered curses and the boots kicked into the ground. They did not like it. Not one bit.

Hruidgar made the sign against evil. As he did so, Brand felt the gaze of Shorty and Taingern upon him. He had told him the men would not like it, but still they had not expected this.

"The swamp was bad enough," Hruidgar said. "Now you want to go into those ruins?"

"Old the fortress may be, but not ruined. Once, as a boy, I hid there from my enemies. I came to no harm. Surely everyone here has courage as great as that of a scared boy? And the walls of the place will serve us well. Unferth will lose his advantage attacking them."

"And did you see the dead men that haunt the place?" Hruidgar asked. "Are the legends true?"

There it was. The crux of the matter. It was almost like Hruidgar was the voice of the whole army, for they fell silent and awaited the answer to his question. But voice or no, it was a question only and not the stating of an intention to resist.

"I saw many strange things. Where there's smoke there's fire. The place is said to be haunted, and I believe it." He stood taller and spoke more proudly. "But I keep my fear for live men with sharp steel rather than dead men with grudges. And they will have no grudge against us, for despite the legends, it's never said that harm comes to anyone who travels by the fortress. Nor did harm come to me, as a boy, within it."

Hruidgar gave a shrug. "What you say is true. Men shun the place, and stories of its haunting are many, but no tale tells of any harm coming to someone. If you go there, I'll follow."

Brand gave a nod to acknowledge his words. He realized that the hunter was helping him, for he had voiced the fears of the soldiers, but then in agreeing to go himself he had deflated any opposition. It was a smart tactic, and once more Brand wondered about the man. He was far more than the simple hunter he seemed.

"We march!" Brand called, seizing the moment. "And if nothing else, soon you'll have walls about you to keep away the wind and a roof to protect you from the rain. He turned and walked to his horse, gathering the reins and leading the army off.

The men followed. He knew they would, for he had just led them to a great victory, but what Hruidgar had done helped. He would not forget, but one day soon he'd have to have a conversation with the hunter and find out more about him.

None of his companions said anything. Shorty and Taingern at least would have faith in his judgement. Sighern, despite his fear of the place, said nothing either. He was one who would go wherever Brand led, no matter his own feelings. It was one more responsibility on top of a long list of others, but Brand would do his best not to let him down.

The men followed behind, quiet and subdued. They had no wish to go where he intended, yet they marched at a good pace and did not let their doubts slow them. They were fine soldiers, learning to trust in their leader and work well together in a single unit. Had he the time, he could turn them into one of the best armies in all Alithoras. But what then? What would he do with them? It worried him that his mind even went to such places.

Throughout the day scouts reported to him. They were not being followed, nor was there any sign of enemies ahead. The battle they had won had given them freedom of movement, at least for a while. The High Way was theirs, and they moved quickly along it.

As the army marched, passing by villages and farming lands, new recruits joined them. Rumor of their victory went before the marching men. And rumor of their victory also brought its opposite: knowledge that Unferth could be defeated and overthrown. When the army came into view, it swelled people's hearts. Here were the soldiers who had fought back, who had outsmarted and outmaneuvered Unferth's army and given the usurper a bloody nose. Next would come the final battle, and they wanted to be a part of that, they wanted to do their bit as the men already in the army had done theirs.

So it went, mile by mile and village by village. Many who joined them were farmers, young men more used to tending sheep and cattle than fighting, but every man in the Duthgar trained as a child in the arts of the warrior and most had at least a sword and helm. Many had coats of mail armor also, and those who did not had vests of hardened leather.

The day passed. Another day followed, like the first, only now they were in a more populous part of the Duthgar and the number of recruits increased. Lords in halls also joined them, and Brand sent word ahead through his scouts that they needed food. This too, they increasingly were given as they progressed. And they would have need of it if Brand's tactics worked, for within Pennling Palace they would be under siege, and they would need supplies to last them some while. But it was not going to be a long siege. The Duthenor, neither attackers nor defenders, had the temperament for that.

The lords were useful with supplies. They had wealth, and this purchased many needful things. Their swords were welcome too, and they brought men with them, though most of these would have joined Brand's army anyway. Many a lord joined the army merely because without doing so they would be left in their own lands, bereft of warriors and prestige. Moreover, better than anything else, the lords spread the word of the army's coming and to whence it marched. They used riders for this, and word spread. Brand was done hiding. He did not care now if Unferth found him. He *wanted* his enemy to find him.

Late in the afternoon, the High Way climbed upward. A great forest of dark pines swathed the steep lands to left and right. Brand knew that forest, had hidden there also for a time. A dim and dreary place, yet he had liked it well enough once he had got used to it.

The road was steep now. There were no farms here, no people, no sign of habitation of any sort. The Duthenor came seldom here, and when they did they hastened along the road, wary of being forced to camp the night near Pennling Palace. And there, at last, it stood.

It was just as he remembered it. Like an outcrop of the stony ridge upon which it was built, ancient, crumbling in places, but not at the walls. The forest did not grow near it, though here and there some stunted trees made the attempt. It was a bulky thing, a hulking fortress, the stone of its making massive blocks that only a giant could move. So ran some of the legends, but Brand knew better. Men had built it, and they built it to keep at bay an attacking army.

Shorty let out a low whistle. "It sure isn't pretty, but whoever built it knew what they were about. Unferth will grind his teeth when he sees it."

"Aye," Taingern agreed. "But for the moment I'm less interested in Unferth and more in who built it. If it wasn't the Duthenor, then who are the dead men that are supposed to haunt it? And why?"

6. Sorcery

Brand had no answers to Taingern's questions. He did not know who had built the fortress, or why it might be haunted. But he had guesses that would serve for the moment. Soon enough, he would learn if his guesses were correct.

"It was probably built by the Letharn, that ancient race that once ruled much of Alithoras. Why? Who can say? It's a fortress though, and that means it had a military purpose. I was once told that the greatest enemy of the Letharn were a people known as the Kirsch. Legend says that their empire was far, far to the south. I would guess the fortress to be a defense against them."

Taingern kept his gaze on the structure ahead. "And what of the dead men said to haunt it?"

"That may be mere legend," Brand answered. "Or it may be true. I cannot say."

"But you have suspicions, yes?"

Taingern knew him well, too well it seemed sometimes. "Of course. If it's true, which remains to be seen, then there was sorcery involved. Whose, and to what purpose, I don't know."

"But to no good purpose," Taingern replied. It was not a question but rather a statement, and Brand agreed.

"No, there's evil behind it, that's for sure." He did not bother to pretend anymore that the fortress may not be haunted. He had seen neither ghost nor spirit when he was here as a boy, but he *had* felt unseen eyes on him and heard noises that could not be accounted for. And the long-dead remains of ancient warriors had been visible, and the relics of the final battle they had fought. No, he had not seen any ghosts, but he had not stayed there more than a day and a night. This time, he would be here longer, and the truth, whatever it was, would come out.

The army drew closer to the structure. A massive thing of gray stone it was, impenetrable and hopeless to attack. Yet once it had been, and the defenders had lost. That much he could read by the damage done to the defenses. He hoped that he and the Duthenor had more luck than those who last held the walls.

Behind, the army slowed. Every man looked on those same walls. They knew death had visited them in past ages, and they hoped to escape the fate, whatever it was, that caused the fortress to be haunted. They did not need the proofs that Brand wanted in order to believe with certainty, they believed as a matter of faith. The legends said it was haunted, and that was that. Yet even so, grim and fearful as they had become, they followed him, and he was proud to be their leader.

They came to a point where there were signs of an old road branching off from the High Way, and Brand took it. It led directly to the fortress. The path was covered by overgrown grass, and stumpy shrubbery dotted it. Yet it went straight as an arrow shot to the middle section of the wall that faced them.

The further they went, the more the true size of Pennling Palace was apparent. It was not huge in terms of the ground that it covered, but it had a *presence*. Brand had no other word for it. Massive stones were laid on massive stones. The walls ran straight and true despite their size, as though it had been mere child's play to construct them, and the proportions of towers and minarets to walls was beautifully crafted. At least to a military eye. Most of all, it was a construction that dominated. And that was no accident. But there were problems too, brought on by time and the effects of the last battle fought here.

"These will have to go," Brand said, sweeping out an arm to indicate the stunted trees that grew in patches close to the walls. "Not an ant should be able to find cover from arrow shot from above."

"I'll organize men to see to it," Taingern offered.

They came to a gate in the wall. A gate was always the weakest link in the defense, and so it had proved here in ages past. What remained of it was a thing of buckled metal bars, pitted by rust and covered in lichen. And yet the metal could not have been iron, otherwise Brand doubted it would have survived century after century in the open. No, it was a metal the making of which had likely not survived into the current age. For that reason, perhaps the gate could be salvaged.

He turned to Shorty. "You're in charge of the gate. Find whatever men in the army have experience with blacksmithing, and see what they can do with it." He did not have to say it was the first priority. Shorty knew that as well as he.

Brand led the army onward. At least the two towers that hulked to each side and allowed men to protect the gate appeared in good shape. From them, men could fire arrows, throw spears and drop stones or heated oil on an enemy.

The stonework around the gate, or where the gate would have stood if not broken, was a strange shape. Instead of square or rectangular, it was triangular. So too the gate itself, but that part of the twisted metal lay mostly beneath some rubble. He had seen such designs before. It was confirmation that the Letharn had built this place, for the triangle was a pattern they favored. The places where he had seen such workmanship before were all of a likeness to what he saw now. It was a strange design to his eyes, but it gave him comfort too. The Letharn built things to endure.

They passed along the dark tunnel that led through the wall. It was a creepy place, full of shadows and echoes. It was a killing ground, and slots within the walls allowed room for arrows to be fired and spears thrust. In the last battle, the defenses had served their purpose. Here and there were bits and pieces of rusted metal, likely to be all that was left of weapons and armor, the wooden shafts having rotted away eons ago. White bone glimmered in places too, dug up from beneath the rubble and dirt that lined the floor by scavengers.

Brand estimated the tunnel to be some thirty feet long when he emerged out the other end. That meant walls thirty feet thick, assuming they were the same all around the fortress. Let Unferth crack his head against that. It was a grim thought, but he liked it. Whatever frustrated his enemy was a thing of glory.

His grim humor was short-lived. Unferth would send men to their deaths here, but he would likely not fight himself. But time would tell on that point. If he did not though, he would have more and more trouble sending the men. They would dislike it, and morale would deteriorate swiftly.

He walked into a courtyard. This too was a killing ground, and many had died here. The remnants of ancient battle were still visible, but on a far vaster scale than in the tunnel.

"This will all need to be cleared," Shorty said.

It was a graveyard, of sorts, and Brand was mindful of that. "Yes, but ensure that whatever bones are found receive an honorable burial outside the walls."

It was not much, but it was the best he could do. He felt a kinship with the men who had died defending this place. He and his army would soon face the same.

44

He swung to Sighern. "For a while, this fortress is the heart of the Duthgar. Climb the stairs yonder," he pointed to one of the gate towers that would provide access to the battlement, "and secure the flag somewhere at the top. It will be visible to the countryside about and let new recruits know that Duthenor warriors occupy this place."

Sighern flashed him a grin and ran into the tower.

"The energy of youth," Shorty muttered. "The time will come when he'll wish that he conserved his strength."

"But it's good to see anyway," Taingern said. "He takes his role with the banner seriously, and well he might. Time enough in the days to come to learn the hardships of war."

Brand did not comment. His mind was busy, for it was his job to ensure that whatever hardships came were minimized. He could not stop them, but if he played his role well, he could lessen the tragedy to come.

He opened his senses to the courtyard and the ancient battle that had been fought here. In response, he felt the magic within him stir. It sent out tendrils, seeking, questing, discovering.

The battle was ancient, but this much he knew already. Death abounded, and the stone paving of the courtyard had run red with blood. This much he had already discerned. Yet there was betrayal too. He swung to the gate tunnel, and realized that it stank with treachery. This was good to know. The enemy had not overthrown the gate, but rather some small number of defenders had arranged … had allowed … the enemy to enter and destroy it. No. That was not it. Not enemy warriors. They would not have needed to bend and buckle the gate as Brand himself had seen just moments ago. No. If they were allowed in by treachery, the gate would not have been damaged.

Sorcery. That was it. Brand's magic flared to life. It felt the touch of ancient magic, both within the gate and from without that had been used to destroy it. It was not constructed of some strange metal, rather it had been infused with defensive magic. And the betrayers had allowed the sorcerer to work his spells unobstructed. After that, the tide of the battle had turned and death washed over the fortress in a mighty wave, unstoppable.

Brand swayed. This was a use of the magic that he had never attempted before, had not even known was possible. But the magic had a life of its own. Sometimes it prompted him, rose as though by instinct as it did now. Yet he had the disconcerting feeling of being in two places at once, and the world spun slowly around him, filled with shadows. He must learn whatever else he could quickly.

More than one type of magic had been used here. The one was unfamiliar, the other he had sensed in different places and times. It reminded him of Aranloth, and he knew then that this was not only a Letharn stronghold but one guarded by soldiers and a wizard of great power. There had been a battle here of enormous scope, and not just men against men and sword against sword but wizardry against sorcery. The memory of it lingered still, after all these years.

And there was more than memory. Somewhere, sorcery still lived. As his senses sharpened, he felt it all the more strongly. Black. Evil. A blight upon the Duthgar. He could not tell exactly where its origin was, but it was within the heart of the fortress, and down deep, deep in the earth.

He swayed again, and felt Taingern's hand on his shoulder, supporting him. The earth seemed to rush toward him, but his friend caught him and held him up.

"What is it?" Taingern hissed. He seemed to think they were under some sort of attack, for his sword was drawn in his other hand and his gaze darted to and fro, seeking some enemy but finding none.

Brand straightened. The magic faded away, and he felt strength return to his legs. But the memory of evil left a cold sensation in his very bones, and a dread chill settled into the pit of his stomach.

"All is well," he said. "At least with us."

Taingern looked uncertain, but sheathed his sword.

Shorty had drawn close too, a concerned look on his face. "Something just happened then. What was it?"

"First things first," Brand answered. He called over some of the lords and gave instructions.

"The foundations of all we need are here, but we must work hard to bring it all into the best shape possible. And we don't have much time."

He told them what he wanted done. Scouts must be sent out far and wide to discover what was happening in the Duthgar. The battlements were to be checked, cleared of rubble and manned. The trees before the walls were to be cleared, and they would report to Taingern on progress. The gate was to be looked at and seen if it would serve again. Shorty would supervise that. He also instructed that the fortress be explored, and that barracks for the men to sleep in and kitchens were to be found. Facilities for this would exist in the fortress. And water was to be located and checked. There would be wells here.

"In short," he said, "make this place fit to live in and defend, perhaps for weeks. But do it quickly. Unferth may be upon us in mere days."

The lords hastened away. Brand had given them much to do, and they knew he expected results. If they failed in their tasks, others would replace them as leaders.

"And what of us?" Taingern asked, meaning both himself and Shorty. "Someone needs to keep an eye on the lords. They've no experience of what it takes to secure a fortress."

Brand sighed. "No, but they'll manage for a little while by themselves. I gave them clear enough instructions."

"Then you want us for something else?"

"I do. Come with me. There's sorcery afoot in this fortress still, and I have to find its source. I may need your help when I do so."

"I see," Taingern said. "And this will be dangerous?"

"I don't know. But it may be. Something is terribly wrong."

Brand led them away then, but footsteps sounded loud behind them. Sighern was running to catch up with them.

"The banner is secured?" Brand asked.

"At the very top of the tower," the boy answered. "There was a metal loop there to hold a pole, and the flag is flying for all the countryside to see."

"Good!" Brand said. "That banner will serve us well. Soldiers will tell stories in years to come of how they fought beneath it. Best go now though and find a job to help with. Much needs doing, and little time is left, I fear."

"But where are you three going, by yourselves?"

It was plain that the boy had sensed their urgency, and Brand had no wish to lie to him.

"There remains sorcery of some sort still in the fortress. I must find it … and see what its purpose is. I don't want to lock myself into this place until I'm sure it's safe."

"Can I come with you?"

Brand looked at the boy long and hard. He was enthusiastic, but he was young and inexperienced. Whatever was ahead might prove beyond him.

"It could be dangerous. Very dangerous indeed. I just don't know."

Sighern did not hesitate. "No matter," he replied. "I'll take my chances, if you're willing. No one lives forever."

48

Brand looked at him even harder. The boy had enormous courage, and Brand admired that. But he was struck again by just how unusual he was. Where had a boy of his age acquired such bravery? And, for that matter, such a philosophical outlook on life?

But he had asked to go, and he knew it might be dangerous. It was not Brand's way to say no.

"Come along then. But keep your eyes open. And if something happens, run and get help."

Sighern nodded, but Brand had a feeling he would jump in with a blade drawn if there was trouble. He was not one to run away.

7. Bones and Metal

They moved through the fortress. Brand led them, allowing his senses to guide him. He did not invoke the magic again, but he did not need to. It was always a part of him, and some small element of it continually whispered in his mind and acted as a rudder to his instincts.

The fortress was dim, for there were many corridors and rooms and none had good windows. This was no accident. The passageways were killing grounds in their own right, just as had been the tunnel through the outer wall. Here, just as there, slits provided opportunity for defenders to shoot arrows or spear the enemy.

The floors were covered with the debris of long ages. The nests of rats and the signs of scavenges were everywhere. And well might they be, for the dead had once been everywhere too. The defenders had not surrendered even when the outer wall was breached, or had not been allowed to. The fighting continued throughout the fortress.

All that was left of those who once fought and died here were bits of metal that crumbled like dust when touched. And bones. The bones were everywhere, and they had endured better here than in the courtyard. Out there, it was open to the elements, while in here it was enclosed. Most parts of the inner fortress were roofed by stone tiles, and mostly they endured too, keeping sun, wind and rain out.

"It's like a tomb," Shorty muttered.

The words struck a chord with Brand, and his instincts flared. It was very much like a tomb, and the dead were everywhere. The deeper they went, the more he began to sense them. There was truth to the legends of the Duthgar, but he pushed on. He was deeper into the fortress now than he ever dared as a child. And that had been just as well. Could a ghost harm the living?

"What are we looking for, exactly?" Shorty whispered. "It all seems the same to me."

"This way," Brand answered vaguely. But he led them on confidently.

It all looked the same, yet it was not quite so. In places, the fighting had been fiercer and the sense of death stronger. It was a trail of sorts, for while the defenders retreated they had a destination in mind, one last bastion of hope, one final task to accomplish before they died.

At length, they came to the center of the fortress. This was a mighty dome, and above them the arched ceiling still gleamed with color and shifting lights from the many narrow windows in the walls. No doubt there were tiles on the ceiling forming decorative works of art, but the dimness and the grime of millennia obscured them.

But there was light enough to see the floor. Here men had died in the thousands, and the remnants of swords and spears and shields were everywhere. So too the bones of the dead. And even after all this time, there still remained in the air the faint scent of corruption.

Brand led them on, and every step was the desecration of a grave, but it could not be helped. To the center he led them, for here was a strange dais, triangular in shape, broken and half ruined, but not by time. The enemy had done this, and he saw why.

A trapdoor lay in the middle of what was left of the dais. The door itself lay discarded to the side, a thing of twisted metal and ruined wizardry. Once, it had been warded by enchantment, but sorcery had broken it. Had it been built to keep something locked beneath the dome? Or was its purpose to keep the enemy out?

There was only one way to find out. Brand peered into the hole the trapdoor once had covered. There were stairs there, and gently he stepped onto their surface and tested them with his weight. They were made of stone, and held.

He moved slowly, testing each step carefully as he went. The others followed him, and soon they reached an underground chamber with a level floor. There were torches set in the wall, held by metal brackets. He took several of these and handed them around. Whatever oil or tar had been used to make them seemed intact, and Shorty withdrew a small flint box and tried to make fire.

Several times he struck the steel striker against the stone. Sparks flew, and soon the fine and fibrous cloth he used for tinder caught. He breathed upon it, flaring it to life and held it against the torch that Taingern held toward him.

The torch did not catch. The cloth flickered out and Shorty flicked it away with a curse as it burnt down to his fingers. Three times he tried this and failed, but on the fourth the tar-like material at the head of the torch ignited with a splutter of smoke and sparks.

When the torch had caught properly, Taingern held it to the others until they too caught, and then they proceeded.

"What *is* this place?" Shorty asked.

"I don't know," Brand answered. "But the Letharn liked underground chambers, and there are places such as this all over Alithoras. Sometimes … the remnants of their magic guards them still."

"Is this one such place?"

Brand was not sure. "There are traces of wizardry and sorcery all about. I can smell it in the air. The sorcery is still alive, that much I can tell, but what form it takes I cannot say. I've felt nothing like it before. But no, I don't think there's any trap or guard left by the Letharn. From them, we're safe."

It was not reassuring. He was not certain what had happened, but just as the men of this fortress had been overwhelmed, so too had the magic, or the wizard, that defended it.

They moved along the path, the light of the torches flaring and subsiding by turns and filling the air with an acrid stench and greasy smoke. They were on a long corridor, and from it branched other tunnels. There were wooden doors in places, some still hanging from rusted hinges.

"I think this is a cellar," Taingern said.

Brand thought he was right. But the cellar was only a subterfuge. There was some other room beyond it, or below it. That much he knew, though he was not sure how.

He found nothing as he searched but more passageways and the remnants of ancient barrels. It was Sighern who called out, having made a discovery.

"Look at this," he said.

Brand looked, and he saw. It was the opening of a passage like any other in this place, but there were even more dead here than anywhere else. Hollow-eyed skulls gazed up at him. Rusted shards of swords and spear points littered the ground thickly. Arrow heads carpeted the ground like autumn leaves in a forest.

"You're right, Sighern." Brand said. "This corridor is different. The fighting was fiercer here than anywhere else, and that must be for a reason."

Carefully, he moved ahead. The others followed, and the flickering fire of the torches hissed and spluttered. If anything, the fighting had grown more intense as it carried down the corridor. But carry down it had, and it ended in a small room.

The battle had been at its worst here, and Brand could almost feel the terror of fighting in such a confined space. Arrows could not miss, nor spear thrusts nor the cut of blade. It was a bitter fight, without mercy or hope of escape. And the desperate shouting and screaming of their comrades would have filled their ears as they died.

At the back of the room was yet another trapdoor. Once, perhaps, it was secret, for the stonework of casing around it was well made, and perfectly level with the floor. But the door itself was a twisted sheet of thick metal that lay in a corner slowly turning to dust.

"The attackers fought hard to reach this spot," Shorty said. "As hard as any army ever has for anything."

Brand peered down into the blackness of the square opening. "And the defenders tried just as hard to keep them out. Why?"

There was a reason, even if he did not know what it was. And finding out could be dangerous, but they were close now to the answer.

Sighern gave a nonchalant shrug. "There's only one way to find out, isn't there? Let's go down and see."

The boy was right, but again Brand wondered about him. Did he never know fear? Had he been stupid, that was a possibility. But he was quick of thought and never needed to learn something twice. It was a rare man that was both smart and courageous, at least if he did not have to be. But Sighern had wanted to come, knowing the dangers. And now he wanted to push ahead.

Brand gave a shrug of his own. "Let's get this over with."

He eased himself down the opening, and as there had been last time there were stone steps here as well. He trusted these no better, and he took his time. But eventually he came to the bottom, perhaps six feet below the opening, and here he lifted his torch high to see better while he waited for the others to join him.

The walls were no longer built by the hand of man. Here, they were in a natural cave. But it was a narrow passageway still, else Brand would have worried about the weight of the fortress above.

He led them forward once more. The remnants of battle were still thick all about them, and it seemed the long-ago battle had continued to some other point.

They walked a good while, and Brand was sure now that they had passed beyond the perimeter of the fortress. And at that point the cave began to widen. He went ahead, more cautiously now, and drew his sword also. Wherever they were going, and whatever remained there after the battle, must be close now.

"The floor has begun to slope," Taingern said.

He was right. It was a light incline at first, but it grew steeper rapidly. Soon, they found a set of stairs carved into the natural stone of the floor. Brand moved down them.

The air grew colder as they moved deeper beneath the earth. Was this a secret escape route of some sort? Had the defenders fled the fortress?

The stairs ended. Ahead of them was a vast cavern, and the light of all the torches combined did not reach its extremities.

To the left were the still waters of an underground lake. The farther shore was not visible, nor was there the slightest movement or ripple disturbing the dark surface. And dark it was, black as midnight. Brand wondered if it were even water at all, but the light was strange and he could not tell. This much he knew, he would not touch it.

To the side of the lake ran a pebbly shore. It too, like everywhere else, showed the remnants of battle. The fighting had not ceased even here.

Brand paused. He felt the spirits of the dead all around him. Thousands of shadowy voices whispered in his ear. They were cries for help, he thought. The skin all up his spine tightened. Why were they here? What did they want?

"They are all about us," muttered Shorty.

The presence of the spirits was now so strong that no magic was needed to sense them, yet to Brand the invisible weight of their will was like a heavy fog that settled all over the vast chamber.

"The dead can offer us no harm," Sighern said with confidence.

Brand was not so sure, but he moved ahead anyway. Having come this far, he must go on and see this through to the end. But he did not like it. Did the spirits yet guard in death what they had guarded in life?

8. The Power of the Gods

Onward Brand led them. His boots crunched on the pebbly shore. At least, where there were pebbles. Most of the ground seemed to be bones, and they gleamed white in contrast to the black water of the lake. Brand wondered if this should even be so. Was it not the sun that bleached bones white? Underground, would they not be discolored? He dismissed such thoughts from his mind though. The whispering of the dead had grown more urgent.

They moved along the pebbly ribbon of shore. To the right, the cave wall rose high into darkness. To the left, the black water of the lake was silent as the void. All around them was a secretive darkness that pressed forward.

And then the shoreline curved to the left. The wall to the right receded. As they moved, a great space opened up around them, and a stele stood in the floor.

The stele was three-sided, and tall as a man. It was a marking stone such as the Letharn had used, and Brand knew there would be writing on it. But the light was not good, and he caught only glimpses of a strange script cut into the hard surface. He would not be able to read it even if he saw it well, anyway.

It did not matter. His eye was drawn elsewhere. If the battle had been fierce in the fortress, it was fiercer here. This was the place where the defenders made their final stand. Bones and rusted weapons lay everywhere. But that was not all. Over all were the marks of fire. Sorcerous fire. Brand could smell the stench of it, vile and evil.

The bones were scorched. The metal of blades and armor had melted into strange shapes before rust set in. Even the walls were blackened in long streaks. The battle of men against men had culminated here, but so too the one of wizard against sorcerer.

Brand moved with great care. Some element of the sorcery remained alive, and it was here in this place. A sense of dread filled him, but he eased forward, one cautious step after another.

The lake disappeared beneath a great arch of natural stone, and ahead a wall came into view. This was blackened and pitted also. Falls of rubble piled beneath it where sorcerous blasts had torn at the stone, shredding it to loose rocks and dust.

And against that wall was pinned a figure. Brand slowed, but did not stop. The others came with him, step for step, and what was before them gradually became clearer. The light from the smoking torches lit up what had remained in the dark for thousands of years while the world spun and the stars wheeled for countless nights in the open lands above.

The figure was that of a man. Unlike the dead that lay all around, scorched bone and mounds of dust, some sorcery or vestige of wizardry had slowed its decomposition. The man yet had arms and legs and a head that lolled to his chest. After all this time, the once-white robes he wore still hung from his body, though in filthy tatters from the withered frame. The marks of battle were upon him. Arrows pierced his flesh, the shafts dried and brittle with age, but intact. So too a spear that pierced his body, driven deep toward his heart. The gash of an axe opened up his shoulder, and the robe there was a mess of blood that had dried to black dust. Of the axe, there was no sign. One half of the man's face was burned and twisted by sorcerous fire. His left hand was blackened and burned to a stump.

This, Brand guessed, was the wizard. And he had died a terrible death. But the worst of it was that his staff had been taken from him. It too had been used to kill him, for it pierced him like a spear, tearing through the man's body and by the power of sorcery, boring into the stone beyond. Upon that length of wood the wizard hung, impaled.

Brand drew close. He saw now that the body hung not just by the staff. Four metal spikes had been driven through arms and legs to secure the wizard to the wall. Long-dried blood colored the robes at those points. This had been done while the man lived.

A shudder flowed through Brand, and he came to a stop before the body. What agony had this man endured? What person could have inflicted it upon him? It was obscene, and Brand felt a wave of nausea threaten to make him vomit, hardened though he was to battle and death.

And then, beyond comprehension, the body moved. Slowly, the head lifted from the chest and burned-out eyes, sockets of dried blood, gazed at him.

The wizard yet lived, and Brand understood the sorcery that had sickened him. It had caught this man on the cusp of death, and kept him there, kept him between worlds in eternal agony. It was the single greatest evocation of magic that he had ever seen, and the single worst act of humanity he had ever witnessed.

The mouth of the wizard moved, but the lips peeled and blistered. There was no sound, and yet Brand heard words in his mind. Not only did the wizard live, he retained some power of magic.

"Who … Are … You?"

Brand forced himself to remain still. "I am Brand, the rightful chieftain of this land. I now use your fortress as a defense against my enemies."

The wizard shuddered. It seemed that fresh blood oozed through his many wounds.

"The fortress. Has fallen. The enemy is within. No. No. That was … long ago."

Brand gritted his teeth, else he might vomit. "That was long ago. My enemies have not yet arrived."

"What then do you want?" The figure strained against his bonds, and the whisper of a moan came from his mouth. "Do you come to taunt me?"

Brand was appalled. He did not know why he did what he did, but he knelt on one knee.

"No, my lord. I don't know who you are or what you did, but no one deserves this. I will set you free, if I can. I swear it."

"Free?" The word was a whisper in his mind, but it was a scream of hope and anguish at the same time. "Free?"

"Yes, my lord."

There was silence for a moment. Brand sensed his companions behind him, restless and uncertain. Could they hear the wizard's voice? He thought so. And he understood as well that this man spoke a different language, but sending his thoughts mind to mind provided meaning.

"I am tired," the wizard said. "And I am bound. I cannot help you."

"I will do what is needed."

The wizard moaned again, a spasm of pain racking his body. "The staff is the key," his whispered thought came.

Brand did not hesitate. He reached out, albeit slowly, and traced a finger along the surface of the ancient timber that jutted through the other man's body.

Feelings of agony and despair washed over him, and a sense of roiling powers. Almost he snapped his hand away, but he forced himself to keep the contact.

There was magic in the staff, and it drew from the wizard himself. This part of what he felt reminded him of Aranloth, as well it might. Aranloth was of the same ancient Letharn race as this man, of the same order of wizards. There was great similarity there, but wizardry was only one of the powers that he sensed.

Sorcery he felt also, vile and terrible. And the two forces had been combined by the sorcerer himself after defeating the wizard. This he had achieved by the use of a third magic. The source of this power was all around them, for it originated in the land itself, and the lake nearby was a reservoir of it. There were places all of the earth where the natural forces were stronger, and this was one such. And the latent power of it was greater by far than any single person could hope to match.

But how to reverse the spell? Surely the wizard himself must have made the attempt? And yet it was the power of the sorcery, the binding of all these forces together that bound the wizard himself, both to life and to death, that held him transfixed between worlds as well as transfixed to the wall.

Brand understood. The spell worked in two ways. It had a magical aspect as well as a physical. By sorcery, the wizard had been impaled upon the staff, and the end of it driven into the stone. The key to unraveling the spell was to physically remove the staff, an act the wizard was not capable of. It was yet another form of torture, for the means of the wizard's release was a simple matter, and yet for all this time beyond him.

Gently, Brand gripped the staff. He hoped that he understood things correctly. With as great a care as he could, he began to pull.

The staff moved, but did not dislodge. And the wizard screamed. Whether the sound was in his mind or came from those blistered lips, Brand could not tell.

He pulled again, this time with all his might. He must end this now, but the staff did not come loose. The wizard shrieked in agony.

Again Brand tried, and this time the staff slid through the stone with a grinding motion. Faster it moved, and then the length of it came free.

Even as Brand held the staff and pulled it clear, it turned to dust in his hands. The spell unraveled all around him. Sorcery collapsed. Wizardry faltered and blew away like mist before a wind. And the enormous power of the land itself flowed back into the lake from whence it came.

A moment the body of the wizard remained where it was, pinned still by the metal spikes to the wall. Then, no longer caught by the spell, it fell to the floor as a heap of tattered cloth and ancient dust.

Brand stepped back, and the others with him. So died, at long last, a great man. Mighty he had been in life, and without knowing how he knew, Brand guessed the man was not only a wizard but also in command of this fortress and the men who defended it. They had been given no quarter, and fought to the end. They may or may not have been good men; he did not know. But they had courage, and he admired that.

"I have never seen the like," Taingern said softly.

"Nor I," Brand agreed. "And I want never to see it again. This was a deed of cruelty that defies belief."

"Then the dead are gone?" Sighern asked.

It was a good question, and it raised others that were important. That the wizard was transfixed between worlds, he could understand, but why did the spirits of the dead defenders haunt this place? They were not caught in the spell.

"We shall see," Brand replied.

They retraced their steps then, and the body of water, now on their right, had changed. No longer was it black, but rather it was silvery in the flickering light of the torches.

Brand paused. The water began to churn and bubble, and he heard the cries of the long-dead. A thousand, thousand faces he saw in the water, arms stretching forth, fingers grasping at the air. Mist rose from the lake surface, but it was pulled one way and then another by unseen forces.

The lake broke its bank, lapping up onto the pebbly shore. The light of the torches flickered wildly, and Brand sensed the desire of his companions to flee. But they held that desire in check, as did he.

Finally, one figure rose full up above the water. Tall he was, robed in white and a staff in his hands. Like a king he stood, and the glance of his eyes was stern as a statue of stone.

He glided over the water, his body unmoving but some force tugging at his robes, flapping the cloth crazily. It was the wizard, or at least the spirit of him, set free. But when he came to the margin of water and land, he ceased to move, and he fixed Brand with his kingly gaze.

"Brand of the Duthenor," he proclaimed. "You have freed me. It was a good deed, and better than you know."

Brand met the wizard's gaze. "How so, my lord?"

The spirit shook his head. "You know so little. Many things happened in my time, but things happen now also. Evil creeps through the world, and it may slither beside you without you knowing it. Even for one such as you, who rides upon the breath of the dragon, the task ahead will be hard. But these things I will tell you, for you will have need of them."

The wizard closed his eyes as though in thought. The spirits in the water all around him moved and flowed just beneath the surface. Then his eyes opened again.

"These things you should know. There is great power in the lake. Mother-earth is strong here, and the Letharn harnessed her power, sometimes not wisely, to defend our lands. I was one who did so. And at the end, I used that power least wisely of all, to enhance the strength of my warriors. It was not enough, but by that act I bound them to me in death. As I was trapped, so too were they. They who served me willingly with their lives in life, were bound unwillingly in death. You freed us all, and for that a debt is owed."

Brand thought about that. It made sense. And he saw how the sorcerer had grasped the opportunity to punish both the wizard and all who followed him at the same time.

"This also you should know," the wizard continued. "Great though my power was, the strength of the gods of the Kar-ahn-hetep was greater. They humbled me, who had not ever known defeat. Be wary of pride, therefore, lest you be humbled also. Be wary of he that is known as Horta, for he is successor to those who defeated me, and his cunning and his power is great. And he seeks to raise a new god of the south that shall scourge the land. He is your enemy."

The Kar-ahn-hetep Brand did not know, but Horta he had met. He would not underestimate him.

The wizard raised an arm, ethereal as mist, and he pointed straight at Brand. Otherworldly was the specter, but the command of his voice brooked no argument.

"Heed me well! This too I shall tell you, third but not least. You are hunted. The Trickster will deceive you, one of the gods of your enemies. Be wary of her most of all, for she does not come with armies nor might of arms nor the regalia of power. Yet her arts are the deadliest, and she can take any form, be anyone, find any way into your confidences. She will make you your own enemy, and there is none greater in life. Heed me well, Brand of the Duthenor."

This was unexpected. It was the last thing he needed, for already he had too much to contend with. But he knew good advice when he heard it.

"I hear you, and I take your advice." Brand bowed his head as he said the words.

The otherworldly wind that tore at the robes of the wizard intensified. "Three things I have told you," he said, lowering his arm. "One was that I owed you a debt. Call upon me in your need. And you *will* have need. Dead though I am, I am not without power, for a while at least. I will do as I can, though it will not be a great deed. This I owe you."

Brand had little desire for help from the dead. He did not think he would use that offer, for help such as that might be perilous, and he did not think he would ever have a need so great as to risk it. But still, it was nobly offered.

"Farewell, until that hour," the wizard said. His form began to fade, and he receded further back toward the center of the lake.

"What is your name?" Brand called. "I should know that much about you, at least."

As though from faraway the fading figure answered. "I was a wizard-priest, cousin to the emperor. Kurik, my name was in life."

The spirit descended into the water, and with a ripple that went out in a circle he disappeared from sight.

Brand sighed. A great evil had been redressed, yet still he remained uneasy. There was so much that he did not know, not least of all the intentions of Horta. What had the spirit said? That he seeks to raise a new god who will scourge the land? It was a troubling thought, and he realized he was playing a game for which he did not know the rules nor even the identity of the other players. He had returned to the Duthgar to right a wrong and bring justice. He had come back to topple Unferth from the rulership of the Duthenor that he had usurped. Instead, he now found himself fighting a war. And a war against gods. Truly, if there was such a thing as destiny, his was a twisted fate devised by a madman gripped in the vice of a fever-induced dream.

Brand laughed to himself, and his companions eyed him strangely.

9. Calm Before the Storm

Out over the battlements Brand gazed. It was midmorning. It was a clear day of blue sky and sunshine. It was a calm day, yet the men worked unstintingly and brought the fortress into shape, into the shape it must have, for a storm would soon break upon it.

Brand glanced up at the Dragon Banner of the Duthenor. A breeze stiffened it somewhat, and the rippling cloth made the feet of the dragon seem to move as though it walked.

The banner belonged to him, and had belonged to his line before him. It was the symbol of the Duthenor and the sign of his own house, but more precious to him was the blood that stained it. He looked away lest he cry.

Haldring was lost to him. She had died for his cause, and not victory nor fulfilment of justice would ever bring her back.

He missed her, and he wondered what she would make of what was happening now, and what advice she would give him. Probably, she would tell him that he was doing it all wrong. And he would listen to her, strive to justify to her every minute detail of what he did, and where he could not do so he would change his plan to her satisfaction.

But she was not here, and he would have to get by as best he could. Taingern and Shorty were skilled men, although they did not know the Duthgar as had she nor understand the Duthenor well either. He wondered if he did now himself. Too long he had been away, and much had changed. His home did not feel like home anymore.

It felt instead like a nightmare rising from the ashes of his dreams.

"You seem thoughtful," Sighern said.

Brand glanced at his companion, his sole companion for the moment as Shorty and Taingern were supervising the many tasks at hand to bring the fortress into fighting shape.

"Thoughtful perhaps," he answered. "Or maybe just reminiscing. Old men do that."

The boy raised an eyebrow. "You're not even middle-aged yet."

"No. But suddenly, I feel like it."

The boy gazed at him seriously. "You've been thinking of Haldring. You blame yourself for what happened, even though it was not your fault, and you know it. You know also that leading an army, at least one that fights, will result in death. And you worry now that you've not done all that you could to prevent more, but at the same time you know that soon these walls will run red with blood. You know these things, and you accept that as commander of an army you have responsibility for minimizing death, but no capacity to stop it, but still you will treat every death as though it were caused by you."

Brand returned the boy's gaze. He had to stop thinking of him as such. He had insight and wisdom beyond his years.

"And if you're right? What is the remedy for my problem?"

"There is no remedy. Not all the ills in life can be cured. Warriors will die … or live. You do what you must, and to the best of your skill. No man can do more. The harm that comes from your decisions, you'll learn to accept. You've done so in the past, and you'll do so in the days ahead. The Duthgar will have a glorious future, and that will be because of what you do now, mistakes and all."

Brand looked away and out over the battlement to the lands beyond. It seemed to him that sometimes Sighern was a stranger. Where had a boy acquired such wisdom, such depth of understanding? Not for the first time, Brand wondered about him.

"What you say might be right, but neither of us may live to see it."

Sighern shrugged. "There's truth to that. But I have a feeling that both of us will survive this. I don't doubt it, for a moment."

Brand fell silent again. He had much to think on, not least of which was whether or not he had missed any vital task that needed doing.

Out below, many men were working. They cut down the stunted trees that grew around the fortress. The work there was going well, and most of the trees were already gone, having been cut into smaller logs and hauled within the fortress to provide fuel for cooking fires.

The stumps of the trees were partially dug out and fires lit around them to catch the roots. They would smolder slowly for days yet, but when they burned out all that would be left was a clear killing field. From where he stood, Brand saw firsthand the advantage of that. Had he a bow, he could shoot a clean shot for a good way out beyond the fortress, and there was no hiding place or cover for the enemy. He wished he had more bowmen though, and ones better trained to the nuances of war rather than hunting. But he had what he had, and he would make the most of it.

Spearmen would also hurl javelins from up here, but their range was much less. Foragers had been sent into the woods around about to collect what timber they could turn into javelins. Ash was best, but other woods would suffice. And forges had been found and cleaned in the fortress too. The smiths would forge arrow and spear heads from whatever metal could be salvaged. In a stroke of luck, ancient bins of iron ore had also been found near the smithies, ready to be used in another age of the world and untouched since. How much the world must have changed since then. And how little.

Brand could not quite see the gate, though it was immediately below him. Shorty would be there, supervising repairs just as Taingern was away in the woods somewhere organizing the parties that were gathering timber.

Luck had favored them with the gate. It looked a mess, and yet with the forges repaired the smiths said they would be able to beat it into rough shape again, strengthen the weaker areas and repair the mechanism by which it was raised and lowered as a portcullis.

Barracks for the soldiers had been found and cleaned. Of these, there were far more than were required. The Letharn had garrisoned many more men here than he had at his disposal. At least, they had the space for them. That was a disquieting thought. Even with all those men, they had still been overrun. Sorcery had been involved there though, powerful and directed by an attacker without mercy. Yet, might that not happen now also? What might Horta be capable of?

He put those thoughts aside. He must be prepared for anything, but he could not guess in advance what it would be. Horta was beyond his control, and he must focus now only on what he had influence over.

The kitchens had been found, and some of those were being cleaned and repaired. An army fought best on a good ration, especially well-cooked food. It would be quite an improvement on the trail rations they had been eating so far, and so too the roofs over their heads and protection from the elements. All factors to raise morale. And yet the Duthenor had no experience of siege warfare, nor any liking of the idea. That might change though when the attack finally came and they saw firsthand the advantages of facing your enemy when they had to find a way through a barrage of missiles, and then scale a wall to get to you. Yes, the Duthenor would begin to like it very quickly then.

Lunch time drew near, and Shorty and Taingern reported on their progress. They ate a quick meal of fresh-baked bread, direct from the fortress ovens that had been fired. With this was some cheese and watered wine.

"The work goes well," Shorty said. "The men go at it hard, harder than most soldiers in Cardoroth."

Brand laughed. "That's because in Cardoroth they were professional soldiers. Most of the men here have to work for a living, and many of them are farmers. Few jobs are tougher than that, and the work breeds good warriors."

"True enough," Taingern agreed. "I've seen the Duthenor fight now, and though they may not quite have the technique and discipline of professional soldiers, they're not far behind. But whatever they do for a living, each of them is a warrior born in their hearts."

That was certainly true. Brand thought back to his days as a child. Every story he ever heard, every hero he ever looked up to, they were warriors all. The Duthenor were a warlike race. Necessity had forged them so.

Shorty sipped at his watered wine. No doubt he would have preferred beer, but there was little of that.

"All goes well, Brand. But are you sure you want to stay here? Soon there'll be no choice in the matter, but for now you still have freedom of movement."

"Are you worried?" Brand replied. "Do you think Unferth will pen us up here?"

"He might do. Once he comes, there'll be no escape, no alternative strategies. It will be defend the walls or die."

71

"True enough. And I don't much like not having other options, but the fortress will serve us well. Away from it, I think I'd begin to miss it very quickly."

"How will the Duthenor adapt to fighting behind a wall?" Shorty asked.

"They'll learn quickly." Brand was sure of that. "But perhaps we can speed things up. Appoint captains and talk to them day and night about what to expect. Let them practice mock battles on the ramparts, and teach them how to use long poles to dislodge ladders enemies used to scale the wall. Make sure there are axes to cut rope-thrown grappling hooks. Show them the uses of rocks and boiling oil, if we have enough of that."

"We don't," Shorty said. "Not oil anyway. The rest we can do."

"And I'll have the archers and spearmen practice their aim from the ramparts and learn their ranges and distances," Taingern offered.

"Best wait until my men have finished clearing the ground below," Shorty said with a wink.

Taingern seemed to consider it. "If you insist."

Brand was glad of their company. Banter was the warrior's way of dispelling tension. He needed that now, for it was in the calm before the storm that his nerves were always the worst. It was like that with most men. When the swordplay began, the heat of battle melted away nerves. At least, most of the time.

Sighern had been quiet, listening and watching as he always did, soaking up knowledge. He was a quiet young man, old for his age, and he showed less nerves than a seasoned warrior. But a strange look was on his face now.

Sighern had walked out to the very edge of the battlement, his hand up to his forehead to shade his eyes.

"What is it?" Brand asked.

Sighern pointed, and the others followed the direction of his arm.

Brand saw nothing at first, then faraway on a tree-clad slope he spotted a rider. Whoever it was, they came alone, and they rode swiftly. And they made a line as direct as slope and tree allowed straight for the fortress.

10. To the Death

Unferth was bored. A while since, he had set aside his double-bladed axe. He enjoyed the fear it inspired, but it was too heavy to drag around. He did not like his armor either, for it chafed and made movement harder than he was used to. He should have been proud to wear it. In his youth, he dreamed of doing so. But his youth was far away and long ago, his dreams only half realized, and the half that were so remained in jeopardy.

Most of all though, what annoyed him just now was the lack of a hall, a lack of cover from the night and the camp food that he would have cast in the cook's face had he dared serve it to him back at home.

Was he growing old? No, that was not the problem. He could still fight, perhaps better now than he ever had. He was still strong, but he had become used to the comforts of lordship. The problem was that traveling, he had nothing that he liked, not even a bard or storyteller to while away the smoke-ridden hours that each evening meal brought.

The army had been gathered though, the full army. Some five thousand men camped around him, ready and willing to do his bidding. That was a good feeling, and his authority was greater now that he wore the armor of his ancestors. The men revered it, and therefore must revere the man who wore it.

Unferth grunted to himself. Most men revered him, but not so his nephew. Gormengil was ever close by, even as he was now, sitting only a few feet away. And ever his dark eyes showed respect that was fitting for a servant when looking at his king, but there was a hint of judgement there. Not open, but Unferth saw it nonetheless.

His nephew was of the same line, had the same blood of chieftains in his veins. He was a prideful man, and full of the false confidence of youth. He thought he would be a better king. It was an absurdity, but a dangerous one.

Gormengil did not know, but his surreptitious meetings with Horta were not the secrets that he thought. There were eyes and ears everywhere among the Callenor, and they served the king alone.

Horta, he did not trust much, yet the man had served him well and loyally. So far, at least. Gormengil he trusted far less. He was heir to the kingdom, for Unferth had not taken a wife. But he was ambitious. Perhaps ambitious enough to attempt to speed up his inheritance. It was something that Unferth knew to watch for. All the great rulers had to be on guard against such as that.

It was not Horta's fault. He cultivated the younger man, threw him compliments and nuggets of wisdom. To Horta, it was nothing but a prudent backup plan. Unferth did not blame him for having one. The opposite, in fact. Had he not had one he would be showing incompetence, and that was a trait unwelcome in advisors. But Gormengil was another matter. He was of the same blood. The nobility of royalty ran through his veins, and he should be above such things.

Unferth stared into the fire. It was a large blaze, and it would burn through the night bringing warmth. That would be welcome, for he found the ground cold and uncomfortable to sleep on even though summer was drawing on. He had eaten, at least what passed for food at the moment. And he had been given news too. Bad news.

A hall away to the west somewhere had revolted. Some traitors were killed, but many had escaped. No doubt they would go to Brand. He had been warned that others might do the same, or perhaps had already done so and word had not reached him yet. Everywhere was betrayal, and annoyance only exacerbated his boredom.

A slow smile spread over his face. He was bored, and he held a grudge against Gormengil. That was one betrayal, even if it was only in thought yet and not in deed, that he might be able to do something about. With luck, he might remedy that situation and alleviate his boredom at the same time.

He clapped his hands together. "Entertainment! We need something to liven these dull hours."

One of the lords nearby kicked the dirt with his heels. "We have none, sire. There are no bards in the camp."

Unferth grinned at him. "Then we must make our own fun. And I've had my fill of words anyway. All I hear are reports and scouts coming in and the whining of the men. What we need is *action* instead."

"What would that be, my lord? Perhaps a wrestling match?"

Unferth seemed to consider the suggestion. "Yes, indeed. That was the sort of thing I meant. Only we need to make it more entertaining. We need something to liven our battle spirits for the days ahead."

They all looked at him blankly. "Swords!" he barked. "Let us have a duel of blades. That will get the blood flowing."

They did not seem overly happy at the suggestion. Not that they said anything, but he read it in their faces. They all looked down, hoping to remain inconspicuous. None of them wanted to be chosen for such a task.

Fools, Unferth thought. He was a king, but a magnanimous one. He would not order it.

"Two volunteers will be needed. Who shall it be?"

No one answered him, and he grew agitated. It was, perhaps, the mead he had drunk before eating. And after. But he was their king, and it was only proper for his wishes to be fulfilled.

"Well? Are there no men of courage here? Shall I send word to the common soldiers for two of them to come forth? Or are there lords among us who will do as their king wishes?"

Vorbald stood. He was a tall man, thickset and strong. He had a reputation as a fighter, and it was said that once he killed three outlaws that he was hunting. They had doubled back and found him without his retinue, but it was to their cost and not his.

Unferth clapped. "I salute you. At least there's one man here of courage, one man fit to sit in the company of a king."

The others remained silent. It was an insult, but they took it. Yet his words had found their mark, for they were targeted so.

Gormengil eventually stood, and he offered a stiff bow. "I too am of the blood of chieftains, and I fear no man nor any fight."

His gaze found that of Vorbald's, and the two men stared at each other, hard and flat. A moment Gormengil turned that gaze on him, and Unferth felt a shiver. The man was cold, cold as a blizzard and just as furious.

It was a look that Unferth did not like. "Let it be to the death then, if each of you are willing."

The two men faced each other again, gazes remaining hard and flat. Gormengil gave a sharp nod to signify he was willing, and Vorbald returned it, a gleam in his eye. Unferth thought the man was beginning to look forward to this. There had always been rivalry between the two.

All around, the group of lords stood and opened up a space for the combatants. They were silent as ghosts, and

Unferth was pleased. This was turning out better than expected. In addition to everything else, he had managed to find a way to cow them. Dissent was everywhere, if veiled for the moment, but a man who knew he could be fighting for his life at a moment's notice kept his mouth shut and his head down. It was good to know.

The two combatants donned their helms. They already wore chain mail shirts. At each of their sides was strapped their swords, and Unferth was eager to hear those blades clash. But Gormengil turned to him, his voice hollow-sounding as it issued from within the confines of his helm.

"What we do now, will give great *entertainment* for our king. But will not the king offer a great prize to whoever is victorious in return?"

Unferth did not like his tone. There was an edge of disrespect to it. More than an edge. But he could not refuse a prize.

"Very well. What shall it be?" He looked to the lords for a suitable answer, but it was Gormengil who replied, and swiftly.

"The axe of the Callenor."

Unferth's gaze fell to where he had left the axe lie on the ground.

"No! Not that!" he cried. "Never that. The axe belongs to the *chieftains* of the Callenor. It's mine by blood."

Gormengil gazed at him, his eyes dark pits within the shadow of his helm.

"I, too, am of the blood of chieftains. Have you forgotten? Or perhaps you think I'll shame my forefathers, carrying it?"

"I have not forgotten. All I have, all I build, will one day be yours. Unless I take a wife and sire an heir of my own. Even the axe will be yours, one day. But not today."

Vorbald laughed. "You get ahead of yourself, Gorm. Well ahead. You'll have to beat me to claim any prize, and that you will not do."

Vorbald turned to Unferth, but it seemed that he never quite took his gaze off Gormengil, and his hand rested lazily on the hilt of his sheathed sword.

"Sire. A few gold coins are prize enough for me. I have no ambition to be … a rich man. Or anything else."

"So be it," Unferth said. "But not just a few gold coins. As many as the winner can clasp in one hand from my coin chest."

Unferth moved back, and he gave a signal with his hand. The fight could begin.

The two combatants drew their blades. This would be no wild fight, full of bravado and rough swings. These men were skilled fighters, and neither was the kind to allow emotion to rule the battle. They would be cold and calculated, taking their time and testing each other carefully for weaknesses.

The two men inclined their heads, ever so slightly, and they settled into a fighting stance. Vorbald yelled, and he swung a mighty overhand strike at Gormengil. Unferth was amazed. He had misjudged the man, and he would die quickly for his folly.

The sword dropped, cleaving air, for Gormengil had already dodged aside, yet even as he moved away, his own blade was ready to drive forward.

Gormengil never got the chance. Vorbald twisted, quicker than anyone would have thought possible, and his downward stroke angled now straight for Gormengil's head.

Vorbald had planned this move out, taken a gamble as to which side his opponent would dodge, and prepared for the counterstroke even as the feint was in motion.

It was a dangerous move, but it had paid off. The sword struck Gormengil's helm, and the clang of metal rang through the night.

Gormengil staggered back, his knees buckling and it appeared that he might fall. Vorbald leapt after him, but even as he did so Gormengil sent a deadly riposte with the tip of his blade. Had Vorbald not worn chain mail, it might have disemboweled him, but the steel links of his armor deflected the blow. Even so, he reeled back in sudden pain. If he lived, tomorrow would see a massive bruise flower on his abdomen.

The two men circled each other. Unferth watched them, his gaze riveted. The two opponents were greatly skilled and evenly matched. He was not really sure who he wanted to win. Gormengil was a blood relative, but he was dangerous. More than ever, Unferth knew he wanted the throne. Vorbald, on the other hand, was nobody. Lords were common enough, and he could easily be replaced. Yet of the two, Unferth trusted him the more, and he was a capable leader of men. He would carry out orders, any orders, without question. And he was reliable. Such men were not so easily replaced as lords.

With a flash of swords the two men struck again. Steel rang on steel, and sparks sheared off the blades. This time no advantage was given or taken, and the combatants separated to think of their enemy, and their preferences and their habits in order to find a weakness.

Both men had them. Unferth saw that Gormengil leaned a little too far forward with each stroke, especially a thrusting movement. In this way he was slightly off balance and vulnerable to an attacker who had the skill to use that against him. This was a worse fault in a fist fight than with swords, though Vorbald might yet find a way to exploit the flaw.

Vorbald himself, though better balanced, was not as quick on his feet, and his footwork and the movement of his shoulder signaled in advance his intention to strike.

Gormengil attacked again, this time dropping low and slashing at his enemy's knees. It was a fruitless move. Vorbald, despite not being especially quick on his feet, easily shuffled back.

Vorbald's laugh came hollowly from his helm. "You can do better than that, Gorm. Or are you becoming too afraid to face me man to man? That's how dogs attack, going for the legs."

Gormengil gave no reply, nor was there a change to his smooth movements as he circled the other man. There would not be any sign of anger from him. Gormengil was coldblooded, and all the more so in a fight. He was ice itself, and no taunting would get under his skin. But he would remember, and if he had the victory, Vorbald would regret the insult.

The men circled each other, blades weaving slowly before them, eyes fixed on their enemy. It was like a dance, for every move was full of grace built on years of hard work and practice.

Gormengil skipped forward, his blade lunging. Vorbald skipped back, keeping the same distance between them.

"You speak of dogs," Gormengil said quietly. "You should know. You run away like one."

Vorbald did not like it. But he kept his mouth shut and offered no taunt himself.

Unferth felt sweat trickle down his back. There was tension in the air, for one man at least would die tonight. But they were in no hurry to engage again, each uncertain as to the outcome. They had begun in confidence, but it had ebbed away as no advantage presented itself. So evenly matched were they that chance would determine the outcome of the fight, and this was a thing neither of them wished.

Suddenly Vorbald charged. He danced forward on light feet, but there was nothing light in the stroke of his sword. It was a mighty slash, leveled at his opponent's neck where helm ended and chain mail began. Many men wore a chain mail coif that trailed beneath their helm and protected this vulnerability. Not Gormengil. Nor did he need it.

Gormengil did not dance back, but rather he edged forward a half step. This threw his opponent's timing off, and parried the strike with a deft move for the full force of the blow could not be delivered. Then, with a second deft move, he drove the pommel of his sword direct into Vorbald's helm.

There was a crash as the blow landed, and Vorbald staggered back. He moved to lift his sword between them again, but he was not quick enough. Gormengil followed through, drawing in close and headbutting the other man before following up with another strike of the sword pommel. This one took Vorbald under the chin, and he toppled like a felled tree.

Gormengil was not done. As the other man sprawled on the ground he stamped on his sword arm, crushing the man's wrist beneath his boot and ensuring he released the weapon.

Vorbald screamed. Gormengil ground the heel of his boot in deeper. And then he let go his own blade and drew a fine-pointed dagger. Dropping to his knees and pinning the other man with his weight, he slid the point of the dagger through the eye socket of his opponent's helm.

Vorbald screamed again, and he thrashed in an attempt to dislodge his opponent. But Gormengil was no small man, and Vorbald was badly weakened. The blade penetrated, but stuck, and Vorbald cried out piteously.

Gormengil twisted the blade slowly, seeking a way through the eye into the brain. He hefted his weight upon the blade, and bone suddenly gave way.

Vorbald spasmed and then grew still, blood seeping down onto the ground from out of his helm. A moment Gormengil looked at him, and then he drew forth his dagger. It had snapped, and he stood slowly before casting the broken and bloodied blade near the feet of Unferth.

"Sire," he said softly, no emotion in his voice. "Death is loosed this night, and ere the war is over it will be loosed again."

Unferth knew it as a threat. Knew it as a threat against himself, and anger burned inside him. But he could not prove the words were directed so.

"Fetch my coin chest," he commanded the lord beside him. "A king always pays his debts. And he rewards those who serve him just as they deserve."

11. Word Spreads Like Fire

The rider sped across the slope and angled toward the road leading to the fortress. Whoever it was could ride with supreme skill, for the slope was uneven, steep and dotted with outcrops of rock and boulders. A mistake by either horse or rider was death. Yet the rider came on, weaving a course around all obstacles and somehow finding a safe path.

"He'll kill himself riding like that," Sighern said.

Brand did not answer straightaway. His attention was on the rider alone, and he was gripped by their skill and their courage. But he was also curious.

"Whoever it is," he said without taking his gaze off the scene, "has great skill. But why do it? What drives them? What danger lies behind?"

Shorty slowly shook his head. "There are men out there felling timber. And there are scouts. If the enemy was upon us, then we would have heard long since."

"I think so too," Brand agreed.

They watched as the horse gathered its legs beneath it, and then leapt a line of tumbled stones that would be waist high to a man. The rider bent low in the saddle, helping the horse keep its balance. It landed on the other side, slipping before righting itself, and then speeding on at a nudge from its rider.

But the jump had caused the rider's hood to fall back, and a tumbled mass of dark hair came free. A moment Brand looked, amazed and lost for words.

"Tinwellen," he cried after a moment, and even as he did so she turned the horse onto the road and raced along it, shooting toward the fortress like a dark arrow with a cloud of dust rising behind her.

The others looked at Band. "She was the daughter of the merchant who owned the trading caravans I used as cover to enter the Duthgar. But she shouldn't be here, or anywhere near here."

Explanations would have to wait. He leapt down the stairs at the rear of the battlement two at a time, and the others followed fast behind.

Brand came to the courtyard beneath the gate towers. The tunnel through the wall opened before him, but there he waited. Within the confines of that dark space the clatter of hooves roared and the movement of a rider could be seen speeding through the narrow way.

And then Tinwellen was there, all dark hair and curves, excitement in her eyes and a flash of recognition as she saw him there.

She pulled her horse to a stop. It was a fine animal, though worked hard just now. Its coat was black, but sweat frothed over its flanks and it drew in long breaths of air loudly. It trembled also, close to exhaustion. Even so, it stood proudly. Brand admired it, but it was not one that he had ever seen in the merchant's caravan.

But prouder than the horse was she who rode it. Tinwellen sat there, her eyes haughty and a look of calm on her face as though she had strolled in here by accident and now looked around with mild curiosity. Still, there was the faintest hint of a smile on her lips. She had enjoyed the ride, dangerous as it was.

Brand stepped forward and ran a calming hand over the horse's withers, but he was looking up at Tinwellen all the while.

"I hadn't thought to see you again, but I've missed you." She dismounted gracefully, and looked him in the eye. "Of course you have. I'm not easy to forget, am I?"

He grinned at her. She had not changed at all, except perhaps that there was a darkness in her eyes that had not been there before.

He signaled a soldier to take and care for her mount. "Who could forget you? But I wonder why you're here? And where is the caravan?"

"So, you care for me after all, city boy?"

Brand ignored the looks from the others. They seemed surprised that she called him that. And well they might be, but it was what she had called him when he was in hiding, and he did not mind it even now.

"You know I do," he answered quietly.

She arched an eyebrow at him. "Well, you have a strange way of showing it. First, you lie to me about who you are, and then you run off without even a hug, still less a kiss."

If the others were looking at him before, they did so doubly now. But he did his best to ignore that. She had made him sound churlish, but under the circumstances he did not mind. Perhaps, he had even earned it.

"None of this answers why you're here now. What's happened?"

She stood tall and proud, but that glint of darkness in her eyes was stronger now. She was not the same as she had been, and he felt that something terrible may have happened. Almost, she seemed to sway before him, but she steadied herself and fixed him with her gaze as though nothing had happened.

"Very well. I'll tell you. Much has passed, but in short this is what you need to know. Unferth has imprisoned my father. The king suspects that he knew who you were and helped you into the Duthgar."

Brand had a sinking feeling in his stomach. He had feared something like this, but it was still hard to hear. It did not matter that he had kept his identity secret and told no one. The old man may have guessed, perhaps, who he was and what his intentions were. But he had not *known*. But Unferth would not care about the truth.

"I'm sorry. That was one of the reasons I told none of you anything."

"Well, it's hardly your fault." The look she leveled at him indicated she was only being polite.

"What of the others?"

"The guards were taken by surprise one night. They had no chance to fight back. Laigern may have arranged that, but I can't be sure."

Brand fumed, but he tried not to show it. Laigern would be exactly the type to betray them. And again, it could be laid at his door. The two of them had a feud going, and that would have played a part in things. Perhaps he should have killed him when he had the chance.

Tinwellen seemed to read some of his emotions. She reached out and touched his arm. "It's not your fault. But will you help me? I have nowhere else to turn."

He held her gaze, wishing he had more time to think things through and decide what could be done, but her question demanded an immediate answer.

"Of course I'll help. Though it may be that the only thing I can do is win the war against Unferth. If I do that, then after they will be freed."

She gave a shrug. "That will be soon enough. They're safe for now I think, and nothing is likely to change until after the war anyway."

It was a somewhat cold response. Brand had thought she would be frantic for him to attempt a rescue, but he supposed that the situation had hardened her. She saw the practicalities of things, and that the best way to help really was to win the war. But then there would be a final reckoning with Laigern.

"How did you escape? And how did you know where I am?" he asked.

She looked at him with an air of mystery. "I can do what I can do, and I know the things I know, city boy. And better would you be if you didn't doubt it."

Brand was beginning to remember the manner of her speech. She always liked to keep an edge, so he merely looked at her thoughtfully and said nothing.

After a few moments she grew exasperated. "Very well! If you must know, I had made ... friends with one of the lords at the hall we were staying at. He hid me while the others were taken, and he gave me the horse afterward so that I could escape."

It seemed likely enough, although there was much that she glossed over. She was certainly more than friendly with the lord, but that was not important. Brand had other thoughts on his mind.

"And how did you know where I was?"

She seemed annoyed at him now, and she drew herself up. "The lord asked me to marry him, you know."

Brand grinned at her. "I'm not surprised. But that doesn't answer my question."

She narrowed her eyes, realizing that he was not going to play her game. Or worrying that he was, only that he was playing it better.

"The whole Duthgar knows where you are, city boy. Or it will soon enough. Word spreads like fire about what you've done, and rebellion rises like smoke from the ground everywhere. There's no place that doesn't smell of it."

Brand had thought as much. Still, it was good to hear news from someone who had traveled the land and who knew what was what and why it was so. There was little that Tinwellen ever missed.

He reached out and touched her hand. "You should go from here swiftly, then. You know what's coming, and this will be no safe place. I'll send a few men with you, and when the battle here is done, I'll get word to you to return. Then we'll free your father."

"Safety? Do I look like I need to be kept safe? I can look after myself, thank you very much! But at any rate, this much is true. The most dangerous place in the world right now is with you – but it's also the safest. Who better would I trust in a such a time?"

Brand did not know what to say, and she softened her tone.

"I'll not leave your side. I'm as safe as I can be, right here. And in turn, I offer my loyalty."

Suddenly, knives flashed in her hand, swift as a serpent striking, the points upright and the blades still. She knew how to use them.

"I'm not without defenses, and I'll guard your back as well as you guard mine."

A moment she held his gaze, and as though satisfied that she had made her point, she swung away and imperiously called a servant over.

"Take me somewhere that I can freshen up. On Lord Brand's orders." Even as the man led her off, she turned to Brand and winked at him.

They watched her walk away, her figure swaying just so slightly at each step, her every movement one of controlled grace.

"That's a whole lot of girl, right there," Shorty commented. "You do make some *very* interesting friends, Brand."

Brand did not answer. Tinwellen had been as she always was, but he had forgotten just how strong her presence was.

"I'm sorry," Sighern said into the quiet. "I don't like her."

Shorty shook his head. "What's not to like? And the way she pulled those knives. Very impressive."

"If you don't *mind*," Brand said. "We have things of greater importance to discuss."

Taingern tried hard not to show any amusement, but the corners of his lips twitched.

"See, Brand? I for one am always serious. I'd never talk about any of your female companions. Especially one so good with a set of knives."

Brand ignored him. If he responded, his two old friends would keep going all day.

"This much is what is serious," he said. "There's rebellion in the Duthgar. That's to our benefit, and to Unferth's detriment. Whatever he does, he must act quickly."

"True enough," Shorty replied. "If we thought he'd come to you and attack before, he has all the more reason now. If he doesn't stop you fast, he may as well grab a horse and ride for the hills. They'll be the only friends he has."

It was good news, in its way. But on the other hand, if Unferth defeated him then he could turn his army on the Duthgar. Whatever rebellion was arising would die swiftly then.

They talked a little while longer, and then Brand asked for some food to be brought out to them. They sat down at one of the rough tables that had been placed in the courtyard, nothing more than sawn logs for seats and a wide plank for the table itself, but it was comfortable enough.

Tinwellen returned, and Brand offered her a seat, which she took graciously. This much he liked about her; she was at home around a campfire in the rough company of men, or in the courtyard of a fortress surrounded by soldiers and the threat of war. But he did not doubt that she would be equally at home in the hall of a lord somewhere, or even the palace of a king.

"So," he said, "what's happening in the Duthgar? Tell me all you know."

She sipped delicately at some watered wine. "Rebellion, or the talk of it, is everywhere. Swords are sharpened in every hall, every cottage and every hut. And your name is on everybody's lips."

"And word of the battle?"

"Ah, yes. That too. Your victory is well known, and not just in these parts. Further south it's talked about as well. Unferth has a man … his name is Horta."

"Yes, I know about Horta."

"He's one to watch," she warned.

"You've met him?"

"I meet lots of people. And I understand those I meet well. He's a dangerous man, in his way. But maybe not so dangerous as you."

"And what of Unferth?" Sighern asked. "Does he march to war?"

She glanced at the boy, an eyebrow raised as though wondering what he was doing there, but she answered.

"He'll attack."

"But has he already marched?" Sighern persisted.

"Not when I left the south. But I left swiftly, and I traveled swifter still. He's coming, that much I promise you."

A man brought some food over. This was mostly for Tinwellen, as the others had eaten lunch not long ago. Whatever she thought of bread without butter and some dry cheese for a meal, she did not say.

"I don't doubt that Unferth will come," Brand said. "What I'd like to know is will he come with everything he has, or will he leave soldiers behind to help quell rebellion?"

Tinwellen shrugged. "I'm no soldier, Brand. But I know that when there's a fire in the camp all men come running to put it out. Else the camp burns down."

He thought as much himself. He would soon be facing everything Unferth could throw at him, and he felt gladder than ever to be behind these walls. But it nagged at him that they had fallen once, and he knew that it might be so again.

12. The Wise Man Reads the Future

Horta sat in thought. The goddess was gone, and his acolytes recovering from the form of possession that she had forced upon them. But Arnhaten were sturdy, and they would recover. If not, then the weakest of them would perish, thereby rendering those who remained a smaller, but stronger group.

She had demanded her price for help, and he agreed. He had no choice. That did not mean that he had to like it, but it was done now, and nothing would change it. He must accept the situation for what it was. Only then could he proceed with a calm mind to the next step. That was the important thing. He must think only of his great goal; all else was of little importance. And to achieve that, he must think clearly and act wisely.

What then should be his next step? He had sent word to the Kar-ahn-hetep, and within time an army would come to support him. When that happened, he would be strong. His enemies would be irrelevant, for though diminished as his people were, yet still they were far greater than the Duthenor. Even if they chose to resist, they would be felled like trees before a horde of woodcutters.

But until then, he was vulnerable. No, that was not what he was. For in truth, there was little chance of anything going wrong. There still existed the possibility of failure, though it was small. It disturbed him, but he knew he was one to remain uneasy unless success was guaranteed. It was a fault, and one that he had never remedied. He worried constantly, even when there was no call for it. Perhaps one day he would attain a higher state of thought. But wishing for that … was also a fault.

Horta sighed. He was unsuited for the great task fate had bestowed upon him. He was not great like the magicians of old. But still, he would not let that stop him.

What was to be done now? He must wait for the army to come. It was true that those who would respond to his call would only be the soldiers of his clan. But that was all that would be needed. The full army of his people would perhaps be enough to conquer realms and lands all through Alithoras. That would come later, when the god rose from his tomb.

Brand, and his tricksome army, small though it was, was what worried him most. Unferth should kill him. How could that go wrong? And yet Unferth was a fool, and that was becoming increasingly evident as he had been put under pressure.

But it was possible that Unferth might fail. Against that chance, Su-sarat offered protection. The goddess would *not* fail. She was wise and cunning. She could appear as anyone. She would insinuate herself into Brand's company, or kill a man or woman who already was and guise herself as that person. And once there, she would poison him with words and blind him to truths.

Certainly, he would prefer if she killed Brand. But under the influence of the goddess, in thralldom to her, it would be close enough to death that it did not matter.

Horta took a deep breath. Even so, dare he leave such a pivotal point of destiny to others? Should something somehow go wrong, could he stand before the shade of Char-harash, the god to be, and justify his actions?

He knew the answer to that. He could not, and he would not. He had no taste for battles, but he must go himself. There was risk in this also, for in the turmoil of war he himself could be slain. But that was a risk that he must take. Indeed, if it came to it, he must risk his own life to see Brand dead. But it would not come to that. Between Unferth and Su-sarat, Brand was finished.

And it would be just as well. Horta understood Brand's nature. He would not like being the hunted. He was one who would sooner become the hunter. And that meant he would come for him.

Horta shivered. He was under the protection of gods, but that would be a situation he would not care to face. But he was making fear where there was none. Brand *was* finished.

Yet still, the wise man read the future and used foreknowledge to act first before potential harm turned into actual harm. It must be so now. It was time once more to cast the Kar-karmun. The runes of life and death would show him the truth of his situation and guide him to what he must do.

13. The Runes of Life and Death

Horta waited until nightfall. The cave was a better place to cast the runes than the top of the hill, but the Arnhaten were tired and rest would do them good. If the omens were bad, they would need to be able to travel with great haste.

But night was a good time to cast the runes. The spirits of the dead were more restless then, more easily summoned. But not more biddable.

He had come to hate casting the runes. Summoning spirits was dangerous at the best of times, but these were the spirits of those magicians he had killed. Though constrained, their enmity was a palpable thing. Once, he had enjoyed that. In his youth, he had taken pride in it, had gloried in it as a sign of his power. Now, it just made him feel old and tired.

High on the hill top, sunlight yet shone. But down the slopes below, across fields and forests and flatlands, the long shadows of dusk had crept forth and stolen color from the land.

It was this time of day more than any other where the Duthgar reminded him of home. If he half closed his eyes, he could imagine himself on a ridge of the arid wastes somewhere. There would be goats instead of sheep. In the distance, there would be the calls of desert finches returning from their evening drink. Perhaps, there might also be the roar of a lion from afar. Certainly there would be the wailing bark of the most intelligent desert-dweller of all, the hyena.

His home was a dangerous place. But he loved it, and wished for a moment with all his heart that he was back there.

He bestirred himself, thinking that he must be getting old. He had a job to do, and nothing would stop him. Restless, he walked around the hill top as night fell. The Arnhaten left him alone. They always did when this mood was on him, and just as well.

The night fell suddenly. There was no lion roaring here, but he heard several owls. In the distance, a few cottage lights sprang up in the dark. The murmur of water came from close by, and the temperature fell quickly.

He would not wait until midnight. He had waited long enough, and though midnight was a better time to cast the runes, he was a magician of power. He was strong enough to compel the dead even during the day, if he must.

"Come to me, Arnhaten," he said. "We will delay no longer."

His acolytes moved to sit behind him, Tanata foremost among them as was proper. Horta adjusted his bearskin serape and sat also. And then he began to chant.

There was magic in his words, the magic his ancestors had learned long ago when the gods walked among men. He sensed that power infuse the words with vitality.

The cadence of his voice was harsh, yet the language he spoke, the tongue of a near-forgotten people who once contended to rule the world, was a harsh language. His dead ancestors would be proud of him now, for his power had waxed over the years and his dedication had brought near the arising of the new god. Yes, they would be proud, but they were as harsh as the land that bred them and the gods who tutored them in the mysteries of magic. If he failed them now, when victory was near, they would not forgive him.

Horta brought his mind back to the task at hand, and he lifted his chanting to a higher pitch. Through him, his people might yet rule the world as once they wished. Why did that prospect not bring him the joy that once it had? Was fear of failure disturbing him now that his goal was close to being accomplished? Or was something else happening?

He pulled his thoughts back to the chanting. A mistake during the invocation could be deadly. He continued to utter the ritual words, the power of his magic one with his voice. His disciples chanted with him, and their incantation drifted up and was lost in the vastness of the heavens.

The air around the hill top swirled and grew ice-cold, and the small fire the Arnhaten had built before the summoning gutted erratically. An acrid odor filled the air, and the spirits of the dead moved invisibly all over the crest of the hill. Could they have just now tried to distract his thoughts and cause him to make an error?

Horta ceased to chant, and his acolytes fell silent with him. The magic surrounded him, infused him, drew on his strength and gave form to his purpose. He sat motionless, eyes open but gazing only at the night-dewed grass before him. Those he had summoned were never visible, or at least they rarely were, but he felt their presence.

He shook the small pouch fastened to his belt ten times, fulfilling the ritual as it had been taught to him. And then he carefully dipped his right hand into the pouch and felt the dry bones gathered there. The finger bones of dead men, magicians every one of them.

His fingers slid among the rattling bones, and he took great care to grasp only some of them. To cast all at once presaged ill-fortune of catastrophic proportions. Such a thing rarely happened, but it had occurred to a few magicians over the ages. He would not let it happen to him, but then again, the runes had a life of their own. Or the spirits of the dead exerted control over them. The choice was possibly not within the control of the magician, and that was a sobering thought. Magic had a life of its own, also.

The spirits of the dead surrounded him, the possessors of the bones in life, and they drew in with glee his anxious thoughts. Their ill-will was a cold caress on the back of his neck.

He drew forth the bones, and with a quick but certain jerk of his hand cast them onto the grass. The runes of life and death tumbled and scattered over the ground, and then moved no more.

The future he sought to predict was now revealed by the agency of the summoned spirits, and though he felt their enmity the force of the rite constrained them to obey.

This was always a tense moment. Three bones had fallen, and each had landed cleanly, showing but one rune each. This indicated certainty of the future. But he must still study them carefully, for interpretation was everything, and the less wise sought to imprint their desires over everything. It was foolish. It was a risk. But he was wise enough not to do so. Wishing did not make reality. Deeds did.

The presence of the dead was a cold breath all around him, and their enmity was distracting. They should be released, and he did so.

Almost casually, he chanted again, this time only a few short utterances of command. The spirits were released, their task completed, and the power that had summoned them now repelled them. The small fire flared and then snuffed out. Horta felt the hatred of the spirits rage through the open sky above him, but their enmity was of no import. For a moment, the air swirled and eddied about him with invisible forces, and then the dead were gone.

Silence fell, deep and still over the top of the hill. Nothing moved nor stirred, and Horta turned his thought to the runes and studied them.

First, he studied the finger bone that had fallen higher than the others. This was *Harak*. It was the rune that signified the dualities for war and peace. This, he had been expecting, for war was abroad in the land. But what could he learn from it?

He drew deep of his wisdom, remembering the lore that went with the runes. War, he knew, could exist without peace. But peace could not endure without war, or the threat of war. There were always those who sought to steal or conquer. If not stood up to, the world would fall into chaos. So, what was the lesson for him here? How should he interpret it?

War was certain. And whoever won, peace would descend afterward. Only fools expected one state or the other to prevail without cessation. It was the cycle of nature. Should he win, how could he prepare the ground for the raising of a god? Peace would be beneficial then, for the nation that survived the coming of the god must be brought together to serve him. And after, it would march across the lands to war again. It was something to consider, and Horta knew he must do so. But not quite yet.

He turned his gaze to the next rune. It was lower, but sitting directly beneath the previous. This indicated a strong connection. The rune was *Rasallher*. It had the dual aspects of mountain peak and valley, but it was valley that showed.

Horta sighed. This was always a difficult rune to interpret. From the valley, a mountain peak looked beautiful. Yet so too did the valley from the peak. All life was about perspective, and the moral of the rune was that the wise man put himself in the perspective of his friends or enemies to better understand them or predict their actions.

This is what he must do with Brand, and he must focus on war due to the proximity of the previous rune. What then did Brand intend in terms of a military strategy?

Horta knew what *he* would do. But he was no general. He would gather as many men as he could and come against Unferth to grasp victory. He would use speed and surprise. He admired how Brand had moved his army with stealth also, appearing and disappearing. Was there any reason Brand would not continue exactly as he had been? No, there was not. And yet, perhaps that was the very reason to expect something different. Brand was clever. He would be looking to change his tactics so that they might not be guessed and countered.

Next, he turned his mind to the third rune. It stood apart, quite lower than the previous two and further to the right. *Hassah*. The water and dust rune. Surely one of the most obviously antagonistic runes in that nothing could be the more opposite of each other than water and dust.

Yet as the lore of the Kar-karmun taught, assumptions were often false. The ascendancy of one aspect gave birth to the nadir of its opposite, which in turn grew and became the stronger. Of dust, all life was made, and back into dust all life returned. Even the dry sands of the desert, parched beneath the blazing sun, held the seeds of future life in its dusty embrace. When the rains came, the golden sands turned green and then bloomed with color.

How then should he interpret the rune? It could mean many things. It might suggest that the old ways of the Duthgar were about to die, and the new ways of the rising god would grow. It could mean that. But it could just as easily mean that the established rule of Unferth was about to be overturned by Brand.

It could mean either of these things, but it stood apart from Harak and Rasallher, and that meant that, he thought, it applied more to him than the overall situation of war and the strategies of war the previous two runes revealed. What was he, personally, meant to learn from it?

Even the witless seed and the dumb animal understood when to act and when non-action was required. So the ancient lore taught. The wise man followed nature's example, and acted when it was propitious to do so. Or he held back and waited and showed patience when it was not. In this way, he turned the cycles of nature and the tides of human affairs to his advantage. So, the more he considered this the greater his certainty that it applied to him, and him alone. It was the answer to his most pressing doubt. Should he ride to war beside Unferth, or wait still in the shadows biding his time until his armies came?

The moment drew out, and he was undecided. Then he saw what he had failed to notice in the dark before. A fourth rune had fallen, and the Hassah rune covered it. One bone had fallen perfectly on the other, obscuring it. This had never occurred to him before, and though it was possible, and though the dark helped conceal it, he wondered if the malevolent spirits had played a part. It was possible if he had not chanted the invocation properly.

Gently, he reached out and removed Hassah to show the fourth. It was *El-haran*, which signified the wanderer and the farmer. The one sought adventure and thirsted for new things. The other grew deep roots and knew little, but what it did know it knew with unrivaled intimacy and understanding. The lore also said that people were likewise divided in their hearts. That they may say one thing, but mean another. Or that a thief may do a noble deed and an emperor steal from the poor.

That the two runes had fallen together tied them closely. Hassah, which was water and dust or life from death, and El-haran which signified duplicity of thought against action, might together mean that one close to him intended him harm but veiled his thoughts.

Horta shivered. His back was to the Arnhaten, but he did not think it applied to him now. It applied to Unferth. Someone near to him would bring him harm. And suddenly Horta understood.

Gormengil was one that he had cultivated. The man was cold as ice, and that was a good quality. He was an extraordinary fighter and a man of great courage. That was for the good too. But he was also the heir to Unferth, and for that reason it was prudent to befriend him. If something happened to Unferth, he must rely on Gormengil's goodwill. But the man was also ambitious. No bad thing in itself, but if he planned to usurp Unferth just now it could bring disaster while the land was at war. And with a sickening feeling, he realized that the runes were warning him of just that.

Horta leapt to his feet. He must waste no time. Already it may be too late, and his plans could yet fall to ruin if Brand won the war and controlled the Duthgar. Then, he might learn of the location of the god king's tomb and destroy his body. He did not know how Brand could learn such a thing, but it was possible. The man had surprised him before.

Tanata was instantly by his side. "What is it, master?"

"Trouble. Now move, the lot of you! We have far to go and little time."

He strode down the hill, all the while cursing how far it was from the village. It would take hours to walk there, and when they reached it there would be no rest. No, there would be no rest at all on a night like this, nor any until he caught up with Unferth.

He strode down the hill, and already some of the Arnhaten struggled to keep up.

"Stay with me!" he bellowed over his shoulder. "Or you'll wish that you were dead."

The Arnhaten hastened then, grouping together and trailing close behind. There was fear in their murmuring, but it soon ceased. At the pace he set, talking was difficult.

Tanata ventured a breathy question though. "What did the runes say, master?"

"Trouble, lad. Trouble for Unferth. But we may reach him in time."

"What sort of trouble?"

"The worst kind. Trouble of my own making. I was too friendly with Gormengil … gave him too many ideas. I did not think he was ready to act on it. But he is."

Even in the dark Horta noticed Tanata's expression. It was not in the least puzzled. The man understood straightaway what was going on, had probably long realized that he had been cultivating Gormengil with a view to the possibility that Unferth may die, or need to be removed. He understood, and kept his silence thereafter. All were admirable qualities and Horta began to think that he had found a student at last that was worthy of the full transmission of the mysteries.

But his mind soon turned back to Gormengil. The heir was in many ways a far greater man than his uncle. He was cool of thought and quick of mind. His courage was great, and he had fighting skill to match it. What he lacked though was experience. He was not ready to lead his nation to war. Nor would he necessarily be accepted by all the people. Certainly they were growing sick of Unferth. Even the Callenor seemed to hold him in low esteem these days. But were they ready for Gormengil? Doubt, hesitation and confusion were enemies. And, if even for only a few days, all three would run wild if Gormengil usurped the throne. Such a state Brand would be sure to capitalize on, and that could not be allowed. Not if he could help it.

The night wore on. It grew cold and cloudy. A patter of rain fell several times, but then it faded away. Horta hoped it would stay that way, but no weather was going to stop him or slow him down. Nothing would, but he did expect trouble ahead. Not that it would stop him either. Not now, not in these circumstances. And anyway, it was about time that the sullen villages saw a glimpse of the true power he wielded.

Horta was tired by the time he reached the village, and his arthritic knee ached. If he was not in a bad temper before, he was doubly so now.

He went straight to the king's stables. These were set well away from the hall, but they were guarded by a few soldiers. The horses inside belonged mostly to the king's messengers, but there were others there too. These were owned by lords too old to ride to war and to their wives. Horta needed them, for he needed speed. And as much as he hated riding, he would forget that now. Time was pressing and he would never catch up to the army afoot.

He swung open the doors, his weary acolytes behind him. The few men that were inside, young stable hands and soldiers stood up from where they had been playing dice.

"A dozen horses," Horta commanded. "Saddle them swiftly. We ride to the king."

The men before him looked uncertain, but the oldest of them answered. His hair was gray, but his eyes were steely. He was a man who had once seen fighting. Horta read that look about him, and he did not like it. He wanted no resistance now.

"These horses belong to the king's messengers. We have orders to guard them, and none but the messengers are allowed to use them."

"Stand aside, old man. In the name of the king."

"It's in the name of the king, and at his order that I guard them. I'll not stand aside. If you must have them, seek leave from Lord Hralfling who sits in the king's hall. He's in charge here."

Already this was taking too long, and Horta acted swiftly. The use of magic was his, but surprise would serve him well now. He swung a swift punch that caught the old man flat footed. He tumbled to the ground, but rose up again nearly in the same motion with a knife in his hand.

Tanata was already moving though, and he struck the man a second blow that felled him.

Horta kicked the knife away from his opponent's hand and signaled the Arnhaten through. "Find yourselves horses and saddle them swiftly!"

Some of the stable hands helped the old man up while the soldiers fled the building. They would return with others of their kind no doubt, but Horta hoped to be gone before then.

He found his own favorite horse and saddled it himself. It was beneath him to do servants work such as that, but the situation demanded it. He was ready more quickly than the acolytes. He at least had ridden from time to time, but the others had done so only rarely. But soon they were all gathering before the doors.

Horta saw vague movement through the crack where the two doors stood ajar. But there was room enough to ride through and nothing would stop him.

He urged his mount forward and the others filed behind him. With a kick of his foot he opened the doors wider and rushed through. There were soldiers gathering there, and he saw the glint of cold metal in the night. None of these barbarians liked him, and they would not likely hesitate to use blades, advisor to the king or no.

He kicked his mount again, and it leapt forward. Behind him came the thud of many hooves. Ahead, the soldiers were trying to group together and block his path. They were waving arms and swords now, trying to make the horses shy and stop.

Horta slipped a hand into one of his many pouches, and he drew out a large pinch of grainy powder. With a muttered prayer and a jerk of his arm he cast it out before him.

The powder turned to fire and smoke in the air. Sparks of many colors streaked toward the men and they jumped away in astonishment, opening a gap. Through this Horta charged, and the Arnhaten thundered after him.

He was on his way, and nothing would stop him, but fear rode in the saddle beside him. Would he be too late?

14. You Need Swear No Oath

Tinwellen had been right, Brand realized. The whole Duthgar knew where he was, which was what he wanted, and rebellion was ablaze through the land.

Since dawn, warriors had been coming to the fortress to join him. They looked warily at the old structure, but men on the walls rather than ghosts reassured them. That, and the Dragon Banner of the chieftains of the Duthgar that rippled lazily in the air.

They came at first by their hundreds. And then they numbered in their thousands. He had a true army now. This was no mere band of rebels, but a force to be reckoned with. Well led, they could achieve much. And they brought food and equipment with them.

They also brought tidings. Unferth was on the move. He had indeed commenced to march from the south, and he would not take long to reach here. If he knew yet that his enemy had secured a fortress, no word told. Still less what he thought about it. Brand wished he could see his face when he heard *that* news.

More pressing was the possibility that Unferth had sent spies ahead of him. It was possible. Even among the Duthenor there would be those who would serve an enemy for gold or the promise of status to come. Against this, Brand took precautions.

The new men were spread out. No larger group that came in together was allowed to stay together. They were watched, and Brand had his own men throughout them to listen and report back anything suspicious. This had not happened, but he would not expect it yet either. There was little any traitor could do for the moment, except perhaps to send word back to Unferth of numbers of soldiers and the state of the fortress. But now only trusted men were allowed to leave.

Against the possibility of the fortress's water supplies or food being poisoned, guards were set of trusted men. Against sabotage to the gate, men were also set to watch. If Unferth had sent agents for these tasks, he would likely be disappointed. But Brand doubted the man had the luxury of time to plan such things before he marched, and may only now be discovering the exact whereabouts of his opponent anyway.

One question worried him more than any of the many other concerns he had. Would Unferth attack the fortress? This was the center of his strategy. Despite the new men coming in, he was still at a numerical disadvantage. He needed the walls of the fortress to balance the odds. But that did not mean Unferth would do as expected. On the other hand, if he did not attack and win quickly, revolt could spread through the land. Then he would have to march to stamp it out, probably to several places at once. If he did so, Brand could leave the fortress and crush the enemy piecemeal.

No. Unferth would come. He had to. Having, for the hundredth time satisfied himself of that, Brand left his accustomed position on the battlements to see for himself the many tasks underway.

Tinwellen joined him as he came down the stairs.

"What now, O mighty warlord?" she said. Her eyes gleamed with humor as she spoke.

"Now, we check the gate," he said.

"I'm glad you said that. I've been fretting over the gate *ever* so much."

Despite her sarcasm, she slipped her arm around his and he led her through the gate tunnel.

"I know you're joking," he said. "But the gate is important. We'll not hold the fortress long without it."

She grinned at him, her teeth white in the dim light of the tunnel.

"I know, city boy. I know it well. But you drive yourself too hard. All work and no play is a bad way to prepare for battle. You need something to take your mind off things."

She slowed her step in the middle of the tunnel, at its darkest point. But Brand had seen the bones of dead men here. He knew how they had died, for he had seen men die in terror like that before. Arrow and spear coming through the walls. Nowhere to go except forward, and men waiting there to kill too. She had not seen that, and did not understand it. The remains had been taken away before she arrived.

He kept moving ahead, and he felt her reluctance. Almost, she seemed to stamp her foot, but he might have imagined that. It was dark. Nevertheless, she came along with him and did not let go. If she was offended, she did not show it. But he knew too well that she was not one to trifle with.

There was movement ahead, and the sound of men's voices. Suddenly Shorty loomed up out of the dark.

"Ah, perfect timing. We've just put the last finishing touches on things."

"Let's have a look, then," Brand suggested.

His old friend led them the rest of the way along the tunnel. The light grew swiftly, and the gate stood there, closed.

Brand was impressed. "The smiths have done a good job." It was hard to believe that this was the same gate that he had seen lying in ruin on first entering the fortress. The metal had been straightened, and the rust removed. "It looks like it's newly forged."

He stepped forward and gripped one of the thick bars. There was no weakness there, and he grinned. Unferth would not like this at all. A walled fortress with a good gate? He could picture the anger of the man building up. It would be one thing to learn that his enemy had encamped in such a place, but quite another that the fortress had been made sound and was no ruin of ancient and crumbling defenses.

"Want to see it in action?" Shorty asked.

"By all means."

Brand led Tinwellen back a little. The workmen came away from the gate too, some into the tunnel but most outside beyond the wall.

Shorty brought both hands to his mouth and hollered to the tower above. "Raise the gate, lads!"

A call came back in answer. "Raising the gate!"

Within a few moments a tremor ran through the metal, and the gate rose on two great chains that disappeared up through the lintel and into the gate mechanism above. The chains moved smoothly, and the gate rose steadily. For all that it must have been extraordinarily heavy, it rose as easily as a man might open a cottage door until the gate was fully open.

Shorty flashed him a grin. "Not a sight that Unferth will ever see."

"I should think *not*," Brand replied.

Shorty hailed the men above again. "Lower the gate!"

"Lowering the gate!" came the reply. This time there was a tremendous blast from several horns. It was a warning for all to keep clear. Then swift and smooth the gate dropped. With a mighty clang that boomed through the tunnel the metal rim at the bottom slammed home into its shallow footing of stone on the ground. It was likewise secured within parallel furrows on each side, greased in order to ensure the gate rose and dropped with ease.

Brand could not have been happier. The gate had worried him, but it was as good now as it was when the fortress had first been built.

"Good work!" he called out to all the men gathered there. "Excellent! Let Unferth crack his head against that!"

The men cheered and shook each other's hands. But Tinwellen gave him a sultry look and moved to press her back against the bars, arms flung out and a grin on her face.

"O, great lord! You have me prisoner now. What will you do with me?"

The soldiers erupted with laughter, and Brand tried hard to suppress his own grin. He moved in close and took her by the hand.

"I'll think of something," he said, winking at Shorty.

The men cheered again, even louder than before. Brand led Tinwellen back into the tunnel, and the cheering seemed to not only follow them but to get louder.

They walked ahead, but this time Tinwellen quickened her step as they went through the darker parts of the tunnel. Truly, he could never quite guess what she was going to do next. And maybe he liked that.

"There are quite a few things I need to check on yet," he said as they came back into the courtyard.

"Lead on," she replied, slipping her arm through the crook of his again.

The next few hours went well. If Tinwellen was bored of inspecting the many things that needed checking, she did not show it.

Brand went first to the various wells that had been found. Some were shallow and some deeper. This was good, because it indicated different sources of underground water. If one went dry, the others might keep producing.

He did not doubt that there had been a great quantity of water available when the fortress had been built. Otherwise, it would not have been positioned were it was. Water was critical to an army, and the original army that held this fortress was much larger than the one that occupied it now. But all of that was long, long ago. Since then, the underground water levels could have fallen. It was just as likely that they had risen too, but one was a problem and the other was not. Still, all the signs looked good.

Next, he inspected the kitchens. These had been cleaned and fires burned day and night. An army needed a lot of feeding, and soldiers manned the battlements in shifts day and night. Cooks had been selected too, and though these no longer wore armor or sword, both were piled neatly in corners and ready for use if needed.

The kitchens had been well designed. They were spacious, and there were stone-lined ovens and fire-pits. Each had a chimney too, and these drew the smoke well to send great plumes of blue-white clouds to hang above the fortress when the air was still. They had needed much clearing of debris though to unblock them, the cooks told him.

Brand toured the battlements as well. These were cleaned now, free of debris and little structural work had been needed anywhere. Long poles were stacked in many places, to be used to dislodge scaling ladders. There were axes also, for the severing of ropes thrown over the ramparts with grappling hooks. Fresh made timber buckets were there as well, some containing water and others sawdust. These were to clean the rampart floor of blood, and then to dry the surface once more so that soldiers could better keep their footing.

Away over the Duthgar everything seemed peaceful, but that would change. In the foreground, the land was barren now and clear of tree and shrub. It was a good killing area. Further out, the pine-clad ridges marched away. Brand's heart was in places like that, with the scent of resin in the air and the mysteries of forest paths that led to the high places or down into secret valleys. But war was his life now, and he drew his gaze, and his thoughts, back to his responsibilities.

In many places along the battlements mock battles were being fought to get the defenders used to siege warfare. What these men learned now as a game, Unferth's would learn later at a cost of blood. He could not pity them. The general who pitied the enemy lost. At least, he could not pity them until he won, if that came to pass. Truly, he had less choice in things than he had ever thought. Necessity drove him, as it always had and always would.

The soldiers were good with the long poles, dislodging ladders swiftly. It would be harder with the weight of people on them, and the fear of death breathing down their necks. But they were hard men, and they understood this.

In other places, groups of archers took turns to fire at targets below. There were too few archers for Brand's liking, but it was a skill that needed learning like all others. He could put bows into the hands of many other men, but ten who could shoot with accuracy and speed were worth more than a hundred without skill. He would make do with what he had.

There were more spearmen, and this too was a skill, but not so great as archery. Strong men, and athletic, as most Duthenor were, could hurl a javelin with great force. One by itself might be dodged and avoided. But thrown as a unit as these men were training to do, to dodge one was to step into another, and to raise a shield to protect the face was to expose the legs.

Tinwellen also took in the training, and seemed impressed by it.

"You leave nothing to chance, do you?"

"Not if I can help it," Brand said with determination. "But the chances of the world are many, and no general can foresee them all."

The expression on her face indicated she agreed with that, but she only nodded solemnly and did not reply. Brand led her back along the rampart to the gate towers, and there descended the stairs at the back of the wall into the courtyard.

Even as they reached the bottom a new batch of men was coming in, several hundred strong. Two lords led them. Their fine armor and jewel-hilted swords identified them as such, but their clothing was of a finer cut also. They saw Brand, and recognized him by the Helm of the Duthenor that he wore, for they strode over quickly and bowed.

"Lord Garvengil at your service," the first said.

"And Lord Brodruin, also at your service," the second added.

"Pleased to meet you, gentlemen." Brand only glanced at them. Most of his attention was on the men the lords had led into the fortress. They seemed well equipped, and they were all tall and strong. They would be a good addition to the defense, but Brand could not help wondering how young they were. Some at least would not yet have seen their twentieth winter, and it disturbed him. How many would die beneath the same Dragon Banner now marked by Haldring's blood? Too many, and every one would be on his conscience. But war gave generals few choices.

Garvengil drew his gaze off the Helm of the Duthenor down to the hilt of Brand's Halathrin-wrought sword. The blade was a legend, but it was a true fighting weapon and the hilt was not decorated in the fashion lords seemed to favor these days. But still Brand sensed a little of the man's unease, even awe.

Brand clapped him on the shoulder, and his companion as well.

"Thank you for coming. You and your men will make a great difference."

"It's nothing but our duty," Brodruin replied.

That much was true, Brand knew. But he knew also that these men might not have come at all unless they believed he had a chance of winning. It was only the recent victory against Unferth that had swayed them, but still, they were here, and that was what mattered.

"When shall we swear our oaths?" Garvengil asked.

Brand was confused. "What oaths?"

"Oaths of fealty to you as our chieftain, or our king if you wish. Unferth calls himself such, but you are more worthy. We hear many things here in the Duthgar, even from far away Cardoroth."

Brand hesitated, and he felt Tinwellen's eyes upon him. This was not why he had come back to the Duthgar. Not exactly. And yet it was his right by birth. It was the destiny stolen away from him. But what of his responsibilities as a lòhren? It was true that he felt more a chieftain than a lòhren, but it was not that simple. Or perhaps for a time he could be both.

"There'll be time enough for that later. In the meantime, you need swear no oaths of loyalty to fight for the freedom of your land."

The two lords seemed a little perplexed, but they bowed.

116

"As you wish," Brodruin said. "In that case, perhaps we had better see to our men."

Brand nodded. "Of course."

They left him then, but Tinwellen's gaze did not. He led her to one of the tables along the side of the courtyard, and there they sat and rested for a while.

All around him men were working feverishly on one thing or the other. It would not stop until well into the evening, and what work that could be carried out was done then by torch light.

"They know the enemy comes," Brand said.

Tinwellen gazed around, and nodded. "You can feel the tension in the air, thickening it."

It was a good way to put it. But if she felt any of that tension herself, she did not show it.

He thought suddenly of the archers that he had seen practicing earlier. If need be, a thrown spear could still do damage with only a sharpened timber point, but better if it had a metal head. The same could be said for arrows, but doubly so because arrows were more deadly due to their accuracy and the numbers that could be shot.

He signaled a man over. "Track down either Shorty or Taingern," he instructed. "Tell them, if it has not already been done, to find whatever scrap metal is in the fortress. Old door hinges, cutlery. Anything. Not all will have rusted away. Some must have been protected from the elements. Find it and use it to make arrowheads. We don't have many archers, but we'll make the most of them. At least they'll not run out of good arrows."

The man went away quickly to fulfil his task. Shorty and Taingern had probably already thought of it, but it may have been overlooked. The weapons and armor of the long-dead soldiers had rusted to dust, but there must be places in the fortress away from water and humidity where some useable metal had survived.

"Will you never rest?" Tinwellen asked, her dark eyes studying him.

His answer was bleaker than he intended. "Time enough to rest when I'm dead."

For once, she had no quick joke or rejoinder. But her dark eyes remained on him, weighing him up as though he were a piece of metal himself being tested for soundness.

15. Dark Dreams

Brand dreamed that night, and it was like no dream that he had ever had before.

His room was small, likely some sort of officer's quarters within one of the barracks of the fortress close to the courtyard. It was dark and windowless, but he had it to himself unlike the men outside who slept in long rows along the floor. Whatever beds had once been here were long decayed. The area had been cleaned though, and the roof was in good condition, considering. If and when it rained, it would prove a good place to be.

With a feeling of unease, Brand woke. Only, he knew that he was still asleep. He was dreaming, and yet his mind was conscious of it and capable of rational thought.

He was alone, and unarmed. He wore neither his helm nor carried a sword. But even as he realized this, enemies appeared all around him. And they each held weapons, drawn and ready for use.

That they were enemies, he knew by the looks in their eyes. There was hatred there. It gleamed in their gazes like a torch in the dark.

Worst of all was that among the many enemies were his friends. But they hated him no less than the others, and he felt the pain of that run through him like fire.

Shorty and Taingern were there, their eyes glittering. But it was Haldring that disturbed him the most. She was accoutered as the shield maiden that she had been in life, only he saw her as she had been in death – vacant-eyed and bloody. Those lifeless eyes still managed to look at him accusingly, and the end of her sword dripped blood.

119

She pointed it at him, and she spoke, her voice dripping with scorn.

"Here is the great king. Hail, Brand, murderer of friends and betrayer of nations."

Brand was as near to panic as he had ever been. What was happening to him? This was a dream, and the people here could not be real. And yet there was something real about it. Some substance and form that was not found in the drifting and random thoughts of normal sleep.

"What do you hold against me, Haldring? It was not my blade that killed you. I would rather have endured it myself than watch you die."

The moment he answered, he knew it was a mistake. His acknowledgement of their presence made them stronger, and their hatred for him intensified and rolled over him like a wave.

He stepped back, and Haldring immediately stepped closer.

"You did not kill me with a blade," she said, "but with your incompetence. You should have seen what would happen, and prevented it. You're a fool. And you're not fit to lead an army."

Was there truth to those words? A part of him believed so. A part did not. But none of that answered what was happening to him now, and that was what mattered most. Guilt could be addressed later.

Shorty pressed forward. He was a small man, but he moved with grace. He was a warrior born, and Brand would not ever like to face him in a fight. There was a deadliness to him, and a coldness in his eyes that Brand had never seen before, though he knew the man's enemies had. Before they died.

"I could be a lord in Cardoroth," the smaller man said. "With a manor and grounds and servants. I could be enjoying life. But no, you don't want that for me. Instead, you drag me to this barbarous land to face death for a people who mean nothing to me. And I'll die here, because you'll make a mistake. You sicken me."

Brand was not going to answer, but this time no answer seemed to be expected. Taingern lifted off his helm, and Brand saw a dagger jutting from his eye.

"You betrayed me," his friend whispered, but his voice rang loud enough inside Brand's head that he would have heard it across the other side of the world. "I gave up everything for you. I, who could have founded a school of philosophers to study the meaning of life and bring wisdom to humanity, died by your own hand. If this is what you bring to your friends, how do you think to lead a nation? You will bring your people to ruin."

It seemed to Brand that the number of his enemies was growing. Wherever he looked, they milled about and cast accusing gazes at him. But he could seldom recognize their faces.

Yet now another stepped forward to reproach him, and the face suddenly became clear, a face he would never forget though he was not yet grown to manhood last time he saw it. Unferth.

And Unferth wore the Helm of the Duthenor. Tall he stood, and proud, though there was an air of justice about him.

"I am the rightful ruler of the Duthgar. I have united two nations, and more will follow. What once was a petty chieftainship, I have raised to the status of kingship. The high seat is no more. Instead, it is a throne. The people prosper beneath my hand, and what do you do to disrupt things? You bring war. You are a warmaker. You are not, nor will ever be, a ruler. But I forgive your sins against me. You know not what you do. Though after this, that excuse will not suffice."

If his demeanor was one of justice before, now it was one of executioner. He drew his sword, and Brand saw that it was the Halathrin-wrought blade that was his own.

As though this were a sign, all his enemies turned their faces upon him at once. And they drew their weapons also, and death was in their eyes. They leapt toward him, and he turned and fled, but they followed swifter than he ran, and he saw that they flew through the air after him as the hawk hurtles toward the dove.

Anger shot through him. He was no dove, no prey for others. And whoever, or whatever, these others were, they were not real. Another thought ran fast on the heels of that. This was a dream, and if so, it was his. If his enemies could fly, then so could he.

He leapt up into the air, and in the manner of dreams the earth fell down behind him and his mind swam the currents of the universe.

With a thought, he was high in the sky, his enemies trailing behind. With another, he was in the deeps of the void with the brightness of stars about him. But still, his enemies followed.

With a silent laugh on his lips he dived down again, hurtling through their ranks and dispersing them. He plummeted back to the blue earth, and there he found the peaks of ice-clad mountains. In life, he had a fear of heights. But in this dream world he leapt from peak to peak with gladness in his heart. But still the enemy came after him.

At a thought, he descended into deep valleys below. It was dark and secretive. Massive pines grew all around blotting out the stars in the sky and even the mountains. But he could still feel those mountains, and their roots that delved deep into the earth, layer and layer of stone and minerals and water and caves. The world, the universe, was boundless. And his mind could take him anywhere.

Yet still his enemies found him, and their rushing presence drove the joy from his heart.

He fled again, this time slipping beneath the still waters of a great lake. It was dark and cold, but he breathed of the water as though it were air and he swam with the silver-scaled fishes that roamed the water, turning and twisting in silvery beauty, their scales flashing in the pale light when they came near the surface.

And even here his pursuers found him. They swam also, and their eyes bored into him with icy malice colder than either mountain peak or the depths of a lake.

He could not escape them. And even as he swam, they lifted bows that they had not had before and shot fiery arrows toward him. The fish were gone. The lake was dark no longer, but lit by orange streaks that darted around him and caused the water to bubble with heat.

Where had bows and arrows come from? If his pursuers could do that, then why not he? It was his dream, after all, and therefore he should be able to shape its reality. Even as the dream-thought came to him, he understood the truth of it.

He turned to face his pursuers. At a thought, the sword of his forefathers was girded at his side. He drew the Halathrin-wrought bade, and it flashed wondrously beneath the water. This gave the enemy pause.

Next, he set the Helm of the Duthenor on his head. He was the heir to the chieftainship of the Duthgar, and he had won this long-lost artifact at risk to his life. It was *his* to wear, and not Unferth's.

A moment later chain mail followed, gleaming silver like the scales of a fish. And finally the banner of the chieftains of the Duthenor floated above his head. The dragon appeared as though it were swimming in the water, and Brand knew also that if he wished he could give it life and set it after his enemies.

But the banner, even in his dreams, was stained by blood as it was in life. There were some realities that bound both the waking and the sleeping worlds, some events that could not be forgotten.

His pursuers halted. At his thought, their weapons vanished. It was his dream, and he would command things as he wished. The Helm of the Duthenor that protected Unferth's head vanished also, disappearing in a sharp burst of light.

And then Brand moved toward them. A moment they gazed at him, surprise on their faces, and then they melted away in an eddy of water and were gone.

Brand was pleased. But the feeling did not last long. Two new figures rose from the depths of the lake, and he cursed violently.

16. Char-harash

The figures drew closer. Brand knew them, and he remembered them well despite the years that had passed since he had last seen them alive. It was his mother and father.

Anger flared through him. This dream was his, and yet he sensed another power at work. The first attack against him had failed, and now his parents were the second. It was too much, and his anger increased even further, but he compressed it into a cold ball inside him. This allowed him to think.

The figures were no more his parents than his previous pursuers had been friends and enemies. They were imagined. And he did not think that it was him who had done so. The dream was his, but someone else, some other force, was using magic to draw out these thoughts from his mind and give them reality within the dream.

But it was a dream, and anything seemed possible here. And all the myriad manifestations of his fears and concerns must have an origin. That they came from him was true, but it was just as true that whoever was doing this to him must also be present, else they could not delve into his thoughts as they had and give them substance within the dream.

Whoever that person was, they were responsible for what was happening, and if they existed, which he was certain now they did, then they must also have a location within the dream, a point of entry into his mind. If he could find that, he could find them.

It was time for the hunted to become the hunter. That the dream was his own helped, for originating in his mind he had the power. He used it now.

He opened his senses. His mind encompassed the dream world, and all that was about him fell away. There was nothing now but the void, and the stars wheeled and spun in the inky sky. This was good, for everything revolved around him. It was his dream after all.

Except one thing did not. One lone star far away on the edge of the sky did not move. That was his enemy, and with a thought Brand, or the dream of him that his sleeping mind had conjured, flew through the vastness and shot toward him as an arrow from a bow.

Even as he felt the vastness of the void speed past him, Brand lifted high his sword and a white light glittered on its edges as a cold fire. It was the embodiment of his wrath, and he sensed the other light retreat away from him.

But Brand would not let it escape, or rather the person it represented. For he sensed the other presence now. It was a man, and one full of malice. He sensed surprise also, and he caught a flickering image of a cave.

The light he pursued vanished, but not quickly enough. Brand sensed the trail it left, and he followed it through the void. Dark was all about him now, without star or moon or the cold glory of the universe. He was in the void no longer. His dream-self had now entered a cave somewhere in Alithoras.

He waited in the dark. His enemy was close by, and unmoving also. But unmoving did not mean scared, or not dangerous.

The cave was not as dark as he first thought. There was a soft light casting faint shadows, and this came off both his helm and his sword. He wondered if he still had the powers of command that he possessed in his dream to alter its reality. Would that work in this place, given that it belonged to the real world and he was only a dream within it? There was only one way to find out.

He willed light to emanate from the sword, but nothing happened. The rules of the dream had changed, because what was happening was no longer solely within his mind. It was different now. Some part of his mind was in this place, and this place was the lair of his enemy.

Brand felt vulnerable in the dark, for he could be easily seen by the light his sword and helm gave off. On the other hand, without light, even dim as it was, his enemy could approach unseen. That would be worse.

Gradually, his eyes adapted to the light. He saw now that this was indeed a cave, though the walls had been smoothed and evened, what little he could discern of them. It was perhaps a man-made chamber.

He dwelled on that thought a moment. What sort of chamber would be hewn out of rock such as this? He did not like the conclusions that he reached. And the more that he began to see of this chamber, the less he liked it.

There was evidence of paintings on the walls, though all he could see was the occasional human shape and some brighter patches of color. It was too dark to observe more, and he was not yet ready to move closer to look. To move might be to die, if that was even possible in a dream. Best not to chance that, yet.

To his right, some bulky objects stood out. These were large earthenware vases, he decided at length. Some were waist high to a man. Some appeared to be sealed, while others were open. And from the open ones he could now see the faint luster of gold. It was confirmation of what he had begun to believe. This was a tomb.

He gazed a little to the left. There was a stone platform there, almost like a dais in a throne room. But it was no dais. Upon it something rested, and he began to wish for the dark once more. Some things were better not to see. But he steeled himself, for he had discovered his enemy, and having discovered him he must learn more. Knowledge was power, and ignorance death.

He stepped closer. The sword he held high in his hands, the point of it just below the level of his gaze. And that which rested on the stone platform became clearer.

It was a body. Ancient it seemed, for the skin, where it showed, was dried and leathery. But the hair that spilled from beneath a strange helm showed traces of color and little damage by time and elements. And the face was there also. No skull was to be seen, but rather the same dried skin as on the hands. It could have been a fresh burial, but it was not.

In the air were the fragrances of cedar oil, myrrh, cassia and frankincense. He had smelled their like once before. He had been in a tomb before, and one built in ancient days by the Letharn. They used such things as embalming agents to preserve the flesh of the dead. And he knew it was so here, also. But he guessed this was no Letharn tomb, but one that belonged to the Kirsch, the ancient enemy of the Letharn.

The body was armored, and a sword of strange design rested near the withered right hand of the corpse. The robes it wore were golden, and the color was evident even in the dim light. There was a suggestion of sorcery too. It lingered in the air, and he knew that some powerful spell had been worked here long, long ago. And it yet endured.

Brand gazed at the corpse. Could this be his enemy? Was it possible? Or was there some subterfuge in action that he had not yet laid bare?

"Speak!" he commanded. "You are discovered, and I know an enemy when I see one."

In truth, he did not expect what happened next. He had spoken only to hear the sound of his own voice amid the crushing weight of the dark and the suffocating sense of inevitable death.

And yet the withered hand twitched, gripping the sword. Some movement stirred the hair beneath the helm, and the face moved, lips forming words though the flesh was dried and the tongue a husk.

Hurlak gee, mishrak ammon hul. Far geru arhat!

Brand stepped back. Fear stabbed into his body like a lightning bolt, and his heart thundered in his chest. That it was only his mind here and not his body did not matter. He knew that these things were happening to him where he slept far away.

He did not understand the words, but he knew a command when he heard one. Here was a man who ruled others, and expected to be obeyed. And then the voice whispered in his mind, and he understood the meaning of the words.

Kneel, mortal. You are in the presence of a god. I speak, and you obey!

Brand felt a desire to obey. Like a weight over his mind it fell, and his left knee buckled. But then he remembered what the man, or god, or whatever it was, had done in his dreams. Invoking images of his dead parents was too much.

"Eat dust and die," Brand answered. "I'm not your subject."

The corpse shuddered, and after a moment Brand realized it was laughter. And then the dried-out mouth began to work again.

"In my time, it was said that you could judge a man by his enemies. There is truth to this, and you are a fitting opponent for such as I. Almost."

Whoever this was, he had a high opinion of himself. But Brand was not impressed.

"Don't enter my dreams again," he warned.

The corpse laughed once more, and it was as disturbing a sight and sound as anything Brand had ever encountered before.

"You are in no position to make threats. Your enemies far outnumber you. One of your allies, nay, one of the closest of your companions, will betray you. Horta will rise against you, bringing his magic to bear as a storm of destruction. And you think yourself safe in a fortress, but doubt gnaws at your soul for you know that it has fallen before. No, it is best that you do not threaten me."

Brand considered the corpse. "You know a lot. For a dead man."

"Dead? You are ignorant of the great mysteries. Who are you to speak of death, or life, or the boundaries between? You know little of what has been, or what could yet be in the future."

"Then tell me this. Who are you?"

"I am Char-harash. Once I led an empire. Once, I commanded powers of magic that would still Horta's heart. Once … but the past is an empty thing. It is a cup of memories sipped from at whiles while the mind contemplates the future."

Brand grew weary of holding his sword upright. But he rested its point lightly against the ground rather than sheath it.

"And what do you see in your future, Char-harash?"

"I see godhood. In life, I was on the brink. In death, I am on the brink of life. In but a little while I shall live again. This husk of flesh will be renewed, this body enlivened. I shall walk the world again, and I, and my brethren to be, will bend it to our wills."

A faint sense of unease stirred in Brand. It was not just these words, it was something else. Why should his enemy speak so freely?

Char-harash, or what was left of him, was not done.

130

"You are strong," his enemy continued. "But you are ill-tutored. Serve me, and I will educate you in the mysteries. Obey me, and the world will tremble at your thought. I can give you powers that you have never dreamed of. There is a place by my side for such as you."

Brand had heard this sort of thing before. It held little temptation for him. What more could a man want but a smile from the girl he loved and a hearty meal? Everything else was empty.

"What point is there in serving a corpse?"

The voice of Char-harash came in answer, cold as death.

"A corpse now, but a god to be."

Brand's unease grew. He had taunted this spirit, and it did not respond with anger. Yet if he was any judge of character, Char-harash was spiteful and vindictive. Or had been in life. Death was not likely to have improved him. Why then had he not reacted with violence?

"You should have left me alone," Brand declared. "No offers of power will sway me. No bribe will tempt me, for you have nothing of true value to give. Instead, you attacked me in my dreams and now insult my honor. And you threaten the land I love. For these things, you have made of me an enemy."

Char-harash laughed once more, and Brand felt his stomach churn. But something was wrong over and above that. What was it?

This much Brand knew. His enemy was willing to talk to him, to threaten or to tempt, it did not seem to matter which. For that, there must be a reason.

A wave of weakness overwhelmed him. At first, he thought his enemy had attacked him in some way, but it was not so. This was something that originated from within himself. And then he understood.

He was here, but it was only his dream-self. Perhaps what some would term a spirit. It was something that he knew was possible, but of which he knew little. And an echo of some instinctive fear ran through him. If the spirit was separated from the body too long, the body would die.

Char-harash was trying to kill him, and that it was not done with an open attack made the danger no less real.

17. Patience

Horta hated riding, but the Arnhaten that came behind him hated it more. They bounced in their saddles and cursed and moaned. Of them all, only Tanata endured the ride in silence.

Through the land they had raced, and ever Horta feared he would be too late. If Gormengil had killed Unferth, the army might already have fallen apart. If Unferth had killed Gormengil, it mattered less. Yet Gormengil was respected, and a king who killed his own heir might lose the support of those he led. Especially when that support had become tenuous.

All things were possible right now, and different destinies vied with each other. Horta could almost feel the land itself hold its breath. He had lived a long time, but seldom had he felt this way before. All hopes were on the cusp of birth, and all catastrophes hovered like a dagger at his neck, ready to slit his throat.

The High Way made the riding easier, if it could be called that. It allowed quick and sure progress, even at night. And it was nighttime now. A village lay on their left as they clattered past, all lit up with lights in every window while the occupants finished their meals and prepared for bed. They were oblivious of the need that drove him, and he kicked his horse ahead a little faster. They were oblivious, but he was not.

For two days they had followed in the wake of the army. But the signs indicated it was close now. Very close. There would be no stopping until they reached it, and if a horse died beneath them, ridden beyond what it had to give, so be it.

The night was not yet old when they saw lights in the distance. Campfires. Thousands of them, and Horta felt a surge of energy thrill through him. He must *not* be too late.

Despite the sense of urgency upon him, he slowed the column to a walk. There would be sentries, and to go rushing through in the dark was to risk being speared or shot by arrow.

The column, which had spread out hundreds of feet, began to bunch together now. Tanata drew alongside him.

"Master, there are men nearby."

Horta did not get a chance to answer. No sooner had Tanata spoken than a group of four men reared up before them, spears in hand.

"Halt!" came a quick command, and Horta sharply drew the reins of his horse in.

One of the four men stepped a pace closer. He did not lower his spear.

"Who comes towards the king's camp? What's your business here?"

"I am Horta, advisor to the king, and my business with Unferth is none of your concern."

The soldier stepped a few paces closer, but the spear remained poised to throw or jab. Horta held his breath, but it had nothing to do with the spear.

The man peered up at him. "I recognize you," he said, at last lowering his spear. "You and your men may ride through."

Horta gave a silent prayer of thanks to the gods, and relief washed over him. He had called the king by name, and stated that his business was with him. Surely, if Gormengil had killed Unferth, the soldier would have said something knowing who he intended to see.

Luck had favored him. Or the quick ride had been worth it. Or, possibly, the runes of life and death had been wrong. Of the three possibilities, he knew the first was the most likely.

He nudged his horse forward without answering the soldier. The man was nothing to him now. All that mattered was what lay ahead, for while Gormengil had not yet made an attempt to usurp the throne, he knew the danger was still there, for the runes were never wrong. And he must still find a way to avert that disaster.

Or had Gormengil made the attempt and failed? That was possible too, and the soldier may not have mentioned it. But he did not think so. There had been a certain amount of tension in the air, but that was natural for sentries stopping travelers entering the camp. Had some sort of assassination attempt been made on the king, the anxiety of the sentries would have been much greater.

They passed through several more guard lines. The smell of smoke and cooking meals hung in the air, and the light and noise of the camp was close to hand.

Horta dismounted. A camp was no place to ride in the dark. The Arnhaten did likewise, and he led them forward through the rows of men. The army seemed vast, and Horta felt as though every set of eyes was turned on him. They all knew who he was, and they all disliked him. Had it not been known that he was an advisor to Unferth, he and his men would long since have been accosted.

The ranks of men, and the fires, and the occasional tent seemed endless. So too the hostile gazes. Yet at length, Horta found his way to the center of the encampment. There were more tents here, for the wealthier camped closer to the king. There were more horses also.

Horta turned to Tanata. "You will come with me when I speak to the king. Stay on your guard."

"What shall I be on guard against?"

Horta hesitated. But the man had proved his intellect and worth.

"Watch the king. And watch Gormengil. See if you can discern how things stand between them. Watch Gormengil especially, for my attention must be only on the king."

Tanata inclined his head, and asked no further questions. He was proving to be the perfect disciple.

They came to the king's tent. Outside were long rows of picket lines for other horses, and Horta and Tanata handed their reins to two of the Arnhaten.

"Stay close by," he commanded them.

He led Tanata to the tent flap where a group of soldiers stood guard. "Tell the king that Horta has come," he commanded. "And I would speak with him."

The men gazed at him with cold eyes, but their leader moved through the tent flap and disappeared. He returned a few moments later. "The king grants you audience."

The tone in which the man spoke was superior, and Horta did not like it. But he swallowed his pride. Soon, if all went well, these men would learn what true power was, and who wielded it. He moved through the tent flap himself, and put such petty thoughts behind him.

It was lit inside by several braziers that gave off a ruddy light. The smell of smoke was strong, and the air was cloying. Horta saw Unferth straightaway, and relief washed through him. It was one thing to deduce the man was still alive, but another to see him.

But Gormengil was there also. Indeed, most of the Callenor war leaders were. They were seated around a crude trestle table. That, some sawed logs for chairs, and the braziers were the only furniture. But all over the ground lay various animal rugs.

Unferth glanced up at him. "I thought war was not to your liking, Horta. But you have decided to come and serve your king anyway?"

Horta bowed. "I am no soldier, and little used to the ways of fighting," he lied. "But it may be, in my own small way, that I can help."

"Then join us at the table. You wield no sword, but you have a sharp mind."

Horta understood what was happening here. It was a war council, and it was evident that they faced some difficulty, judging from the looks on their faces. He glanced carefully at Gormengil as he sat, for he was the one whose emotions must be gauged most, but typically for the man, he was the one who masked what he felt the best. His face may as well have been carved from stone.

Horta was not comfortable on a sawed log for a seat. He would have preferred to sit on the ground. This, at least, Tanata was able to do, and he took up a position close behind him. No one at the table even looked at him. It was a slight, but these barbarians knew nothing of civilized ways. To slight the servant was to slight the master.

Despite his discomfort, Horta listened carefully as the king spoke.

"Brand has dug himself into a hole like a rat." The words were for Horta, bringing him up to date with what the others in the room already knew. "He has occupied an ancient fortress called Pennling Palace. It's a wretched dump, falling apart and reputed to be haunted, but he thinks the walls will keep me from him."

Horta knew the place. His wanderings had taken him across the Duthgar, but he had never ventured inside. The place had a bad reputation, and there was something about it that triggered his instincts.

Gormengil leaned forward, resting his elbows on the table where he sat next to the king.

"The fortress is old," he said, "and I've not been inside. But the walls are still standing, and they are strong."

Unferth grunted. "I don't care about walls and gates. We have the greater army. We'll storm the walls and demolish whatever barricade they've put up for a gate."

"It's not that simple, my king," Gormengil said. "The walls are an advantage to the enemy. And it's clear that Brand isn't going anywhere, so we may as well take the time to gather more men. Then we can be sure of defeating him."

Horta understood. The runes had been right, and Brand had done the unexpected. He also understood that the king's advisors were divided in how they should react. Worst of all, Unferth and Gormengil were on opposite sides of that divide.

Unferth seemed angry. "It's as simple as I say it is. My army outnumbers his. The walls offer a barrier, but they'll not stop me from crushing him, and all who support him."

The reply Gormengil gave was softly spoken, and his voice was void of emotion. But still Horta's blood ran cold to hear him speak.

"You underestimate Brand. You always have, otherwise he would already be dead. I urge you, don't take his skill as a general cheaply this time. Gather more men. Take your time. Be sure of victory before you rush in, foolishly."

Unferth went white. Then his face blossomed red in rage. He stood, and with a casual movement backhanded Gormengil. It was unexpected, and the sudden violence caused men to reel back off their seats and stagger upright.

Gormengil fell to the ground, but then he rose in a smooth motion, his body swaying to and fro like a rearing serpent. It was not dizziness that made him move so, but a martial technique to help avoid being struck while rising from the ground. Horta knew a great fighter when he saw one, and he increased his estimate of Gormengil. And even struck down, the man's face showed no emotion, but his eyes were cold as death.

Gormengil had his right hand on his sword hilt. Unferth reached for the wicked-looking axe he now carried with him. The men around the table stepped further back.

Horta acted swiftly. He drew powder from one of his pouches, and cast it onto the table where it exploded in flashes of multicolored sparks. Then swifter than either the king or the heir he moved, leaping across the table and gripping Gormengil's wrist.

"Stay!" he commanded. "Discord among us is to Brand's favor. Are you all children to squabble while the realm falls around you?"

No one answered. Slowly, Gormengil released his grip on the sword hilt. Unferth seemed in a rage, but he blinked a few times and then his eyes focused on Horta.

"Children, are we? Is that how you speak to your king?"

"I speak the truth," Horta answered. "And you know it. If you wish lickspittles to serve you, too scared to voice an opinion, then strike off my head now. Otherwise, heed my words!"

A long moment Unferth looked at him. "You are more than you seem. But you're right. Discord among us is only to Brand's advantage." He deliberately avoided looking at Gormengil as he spoke, but his gaze flickered to the man at the last and his hands still tightly gripped the haft of the axe.

Horta bowed. "Let me take Gormengil aside, sire. I'll teach him of my wisdom. And then let me speak with you. I sense the magic of Brand at work, sowing disharmony among us." It was not true, but Unferth did not know that, and it would distract him from Gormengil.

Unferth gave a nod of approval, and Horta drew the heir to the throne away. They walked out of the tent and into the semi-dark of the camp. Horta hesitated, and then led the younger man to the picket line of horses where they could speak without being overheard.

Horta swung toward him. "Are you a fool? We've discussed much, and one day you'll be king, but you're not ready yet. If you're not careful, Unferth will have you killed and your dreams will be dust."

The dark eyes of Gormengil gazed back at him, unblinking. "We've discussed many things. Some of it treasonous. You know that as well as I. Yet all I did tonight was offer good counsel to the king."

"It's not what you said. It's how you said it. He knows you wish the throne. He knows you hold him in contempt. Wait. Bide your time. Strike when you're ready and sure of victory. That's what I counsel you. Is it not what you advised the king to do? If you'll not listen to me, will you not at least follow your own polices?"

Gormengil turned away. It was hard to read his face in the shadows, but Horta knew his words had struck home.

"I'm not a hasty man," Gormengil said quietly. "But my dreams are afire with thoughts of kingship. Unferth is a fool. I would be a far better king."

"And so you will be. But now isn't the time for a change of leadership. Not during the middle of a war. Wait until afterward. And who knows, the kingship may come to you naturally if Unferth is killed during battle."

"I too may be killed in battle."

Horta turned away now. He knew something of the future, and something of the plans of the gods, but not enough.

"Patience rewards us all, Gormengil. Wait on your destiny. It will come. Glory, riches and power will soon fill the Duthgar. A nation will rise here to conquer the world, and the leader of the realm will be a god."

Horta looked intently at the other man to assure him he was speaking the truth. It did not matter that he had once had the same conversation with Unferth. What he said was true, and if they believed themselves to be the leader he spoke of, it was not his fault.

18. If I Don't, Who Will?

The dream-spirit that was Brand leapt out of the tomb of Char-harash. But his enemy was guileful and full of malice.

With a flick of his withered hand, the sorcerer sent Brand tumbling into the void, lost and without bearings. The shock of the power used to do so was awesome, and Brand felt fear run through him.

In the void, all was dark and the glitter of faraway stars faint and unfamiliar. Somewhere, he felt his body grow cold, and the blood in his veins begin to turn sluggish. He was near to death, and panic took him.

But he was a warrior. Death, and the threat of death, were familiar feelings. He calmed himself and thought. One thing he realized straightaway. Char-harash, for all his power and seeming familiarity with this dream world, had not followed him. Could it be that he was scared? That was good to know.

Another thought occurred to him. He had no idea where he was, neither his dream-self nor his body, and yet he could still feel his body weakening. He was linked to it in some way. And if that was so, then did he have to find his way back by landmarks or reasoning?

He closed off all his senses and floated in the void, drifting in the great dark. But he concentrated on the vague sensations of his weakening body. Those sensations sharpened, and it felt as though some invisible current within the void had taken him. He no longer drifted aimlessly, but now felt himself pulled in a specific direction.

He willed himself to go that way, and suddenly it felt as though he was falling. The void exploded all around him in shifting colors and burning suns, and he plummeted ever faster through the dreamworld.

Consciousness sped from him, and darkness blanketed his mind. But he woke moments later, his body wracked by pain. He reared up from his makeshift bed in his room in the barracks, gasping for air and shivering with cold. The room spun around him, and he felt violently ill.

He lowered himself back down, shivering and trembling all over. But slowly, his breathing returned to normal and the cold sweat that slicked his skin dried away. All the while, he dared not close his eyes nor even blink except when he must for fear of slipping away into death. He had been close.

It was time to think, and he lay there, eyes open in the dark of his room, doing just that. It was clear now that he must do more than depose Unferth. The Usurper was almost irrelevant in a way. A much larger game was afoot, and greater enemies stalked him. But still, Unferth must be defeated first. Everything, even the greatest of tasks, was accomplished one step at a time. Especially the greatest of tasks. And Unferth was linked with these other threats. His power was the greater because of it, and not just because of the magician Horta. He had been confident in the fortress until now, but a battle was being fought and swords and courage and strategy were not the only factors. Magicians, and gods, and men who wanted to be gods were now a part of the game. How could he defeat them all?

He knew the answer. At least, he knew one way to try, one way that he might bring the odds back to something approaching even. Kurik had told him he would need help. The wizard-priest had offered it. Brand had wanted no part of help from a dead man, from a spirit bound to

143

the world in torture and perhaps in lust for revenge, but now … now he must needs take all the help he could get. If it was not too late. Kurik had warned him that his spirit would not remain in the world for long after his release from the spell that bound him.

It was a task that could not wait, though Brand did not relish it. He stood on shaky legs and dressed. His helm he left behind, but his sword he belted to his waist. Even in a fortress held by his own army it was wise to be prepared. Then he moved silently through the barracks and deeper into the fortress.

He was glad to have the sword, for he felt from early on that someone was following him. He should make his way back to the soldiers while he could and get help. But if he did that, whoever followed him might slip away and remain unknown. It was better to go ahead and see if he could trap them. Knowledge was power, and ignorance death.

He moved ahead. The ways were dark, but he found a torch in a corridor and took it with him. It provided not just light, but would also serve as a weapon.

Down he went, into the depths of the fortress. And his stalker came with him. Whoever it was moved near silently, but not quite silent enough. No one could move silently in such a place of stone and corridors that took sound and threw it around from wall to wall. He made no effort to move quietly himself. Doing so would only serve to warn the person who followed that he was being cautious.

He reached the underground cavern where the body of water lay to his left. There, on the softer ground, he could move silently, and he ran ahead, wedging the torch into some sand and then running back into the shadows. Whoever followed would pause, not wishing to get too close to the light but probably not being able to see that no one held the torch up.

Brand drew his sword and squatted low to the ground. He held the blade behind him so that no flicker of light glimmered from its surface, and he kept his head down. It was the skin of a man's face that often revealed him in the dark, for being paler than his clothes it was more easily seen.

He waited several tense moments, slowing his breathing as much as he could so that he could not be heard. Whoever followed him came forward more quickly than he had guessed. They were sure of themselves to follow so closely, and such confidence spoke of skill. Then again, it could be overconfidence as well.

A shadow moved before him, dark as the perpetual night in this cave. And then it came to a stop. A moment it hesitated, and Brand tensed.

But before he could act, he heard a slow laugh that he knew well.

"Stand up, Brand. I see you there. You would not attack me, would you?"

It was Tinwellen, and Brand was amazed at her courage but also angry at her following him.

He stood and moved toward her. "How did you even see me?"

She laughed softly again, and her hands moved in the dark, perhaps sheathing her knives. "Is it just me you underestimate? Or is it all women? Don't you know that girls see better in the dark than boys?" She hesitated, and then added, "I can show you exactly how well I see in the dark, if you like. That might be fun."

Brand could see the flash of her brilliant smile clearly amid the shadows and his anger evaporated. "Hopefully, I underestimate no one. But why on earth did you follow me? What I do down here could be dangerous."

"Why must I keep telling you this? I have your back."

It was a simple answer, and a powerful one. But she spoke again before he could reply.

"What *are* you doing down here, anyway?" She looked around distastefully at what could be seen of their surroundings.

He told her then all about Kurik, and what had happened here before. And especially about the spirit's offer to help, and why he thought he needed it now.

"You worry too much," was all she said.

"It's my job to worry. If I don't, who will?"

"Things will sort themselves out. You were right to refuse help the first time. Who wants help from a ghost? And how far can you trust him? Better to leave well enough alone. Come back up to the fortress with me and I'll take your mind off all your worries."

He did not doubt that she would do that, and more. But the stakes had grown too high now. He could not turn away an offer for help. Other people would pay for any such mistake as that, and he already had enough on his conscience.

"You go back up. I have business here that I cannot put aside."

She stamped her foot. "I'm not going anywhere, except with you. If you'll not listen to reason, then I guess I'll just have to keep watching your back. Otherwise anything could happen to you down here and no one in the world would know."

That much was true, and not for the first time he wished that he had found Taingern and Shorty before rushing down here.

But all he said though was a simple thank you to Tinwellen. "I appreciate your coming with me. But the night moves on, and I have a feeling that time is running out."

146

He led her forward then. Deftly, he picked up the torch and then proceeded along the edge of the water into the next chamber.

"This was where he was bound," he whispered to Tinwellen.

She looked around, and her eyes gleamed in the torch light, but she said nothing.

"Kurik!" Brand called. "Can you hear me? I would speak with you again."

He knew there were rites involved with summoning the dead, but he did not know what they were, or want to know. But what he did now was no summoning. Either the spirit of Kurik yet lingered in this world, or it did not. Either it would help, or it would not. Both were beyond his control.

For long moments, nothing changed. Then the dark grew darker, and the shadows thicker. The torch in Brand's hand still burned, but it seemed that its flame gave neither light nor warmth. The smoke coiling from it filled the air, spilling out to cover the floor of the chamber.

The smoke before Brand swirled and eddied. Then it took shape, forming the image of a man. It was Kurik, or the spirit of him at least.

"Hail, Brand of the Duthenor. You have called upon me, as I knew you must."

Brand gave a bow. "Hail, my lord. Your wisdom is greater than mine. You offered help, and I spurned it. Now I see better why it is needed. And, if you are still willing, I will accept it."

Kurik made no answer. It seemed as though he was deep in thought. Perhaps that was so. Or perhaps he saw some vision of the future. But after a moment his head came up and his eyes, dark shadows that they were, blazed.

"My help you have requested. And you shall have it, such as it is. My power is spent, and my time nearly gone.

Yet still I may avail you aid, though it is but the shadow of what once I could have done."

"And what will you do, my lord?"

Kurik gazed at him, and then he turned those shadowy eyes upon Tinwellen. A while he studied her, and she returned his gaze without fear. At that moment Brand was proud of her, for few in her position could have done the same.

The spirit turned again to Brand. "I will do what I can, little though it be. But it is best you don't know what it is. The future is dark and untrodden. A misstep now could put you on the wrong path. I dare not risk that. But remember my warnings from when first we met. Keep them close to your heart, and keep hope also. You will need it."

The spirit of the dead man faded away as a movement of air pulled apart the smoke. It was not reassuring to Brand. He needed help, but what help could be given by a dead person whose ghost was not able to withstand a breeze? Yet still, it did not pay to underestimate anybody.

Tinwellen sniffed. "He seemed a stuffy old man to me. He'll be no help to you at all. And why on earth do you call him lord?"

Brand grinned at her. "I call him lord because it seems to me that he deserves it. As for help, time will tell what form it takes."

She frowned at him. "Why are you smiling?"

"Because you're here. Who else would stare back at the spirit of a dead man and call him stuffy after he was gone? Others would have fled, screaming."

That was the type of thing she seemed to want to hear, for her eyes sparked and her smile dazzled him.

"I told you. I have your back. I'm not going anywhere."

"And I have yours."

They retraced their steps up into the fortress then. All the while Brand considered how lucky he was. His friends had always been few, but they were people of character and strength. None more so than Tinwellen.

19. The Breath of the Dragon

Horta slept, but it was a restless sleep troubled by strange dreams. And then the goddess Su-sarat came to him, and she spoke.

"Wake, Horta."

And he woke, yet still remained in the dream. He was in the desert, in a place that he knew of old as a youth. Here he had hunted and ridden his chariot. In this place he had met his first great love, and here he had lost her also. It was dark, and he could see little, but each ridge and hill, each sweep of arid land and stunted bush, he knew them all, knew where they were in the dark even if he could not see them. And the scent of the desert air at night was like wine that intoxicated him.

The voice of the goddess whispered to him out of that darkness. "Horta, Unferth does not sleep and I cannot enter his mind. But I must learn of his plans. Speak to me."

Horta cast his gaze about. The goddess was nowhere to be seen, yet she was everywhere. Never had one of the gods visited him thus, nor had he heard of something similar from another magician.

"I am your servant, Su-sarat. Ask, and I will obey."

He did not like this. There was no ritual to follow here, no way to know if he was saying or doing the right thing.

Her voice came again out of the night. "Will Unferth attack the fortress, or will he wait?"

"He will attack, Great Mistress. Fear drives him, and his hatred for Brand also. He will attack, and he will throw all that he has against the enemy."

The night was still, thoughtful almost. "And his army is great? It will succeed?"

"How can it not?"

The goddess did not answer that. But she did speak again.

"And how long before Unferth reaches the fortress?"

"Soon, O Holy One. It will be soon. If not tomorrow, then the day after."

To this, she offered no answer, but her presence remained all around him. The air throbbed with it. So he risked voicing a question of his own.

"Has Brand fallen into your thrall yet?"

The brooding air about him tensed, and he guessed his mistake. Maybe. He should have given her one of her titles. The gods liked them.

"He resists me, even though he does not know why he does so. It is … desirable. Yet I shall have him in the end and that end is close. I am nearly there."

"Who are you in his group, O Dancer in the Night?" He gave her the title the lore said she liked most. But the lore was not always right.

"It does not matter," she answered. "I could be anyone, and my influence is hidden. That is all you need to know, magician."

He pondered that answer. The word *magician* had been a rebuke. It was meant to put him in his place, and he knew it. His role was one of servant and not questioner.

"I am blessed, O Queen of Secrets," he intoned, "to hear your words. Your will is supreme, your desires will come to fruition. You are a god, and the world orders itself to your thought. I am but a humble servant, and I would draw on your wisdom if I may?"

"Sweet are your words, Horta. Even if they are flattery. But you have earned something at least from me. Ask, and I will give answer."

Horta bowed. But he spoke swiftly. When a god gave permission to do something, it was best to take them up on it straightaway.

"Gormengil, heir to the throne, is a man of immense ambition. I believe he will attempt to displace Unferth. This could be disastrous at the moment, but I fear he may act despite my urgings not to."

"And your question, Horta?"

"Simply this. Should I kill him?"

The presence around him stirred, as though in thought.

"You would already have killed him, had that been best. You keep him alive, because in the future he is one who would serve Char-harash better than Unferth."

She made it a statement, rather than a question.

"That is exactly so, O Holy One."

The night deepened around him. He sensed doubt, fleeting but present. Then it was masked. He hoped the goddess had not realized he sensed it, for that might be his own death. But it troubled him that there should be any doubt at all. The gods were always sure of themselves.

"This Gormengil feels it," she said at last. "The breath of the dragon blows over the land. Change lurks in every shadow. Possibility stirs everywhere, and none know for sure what will be. But in the end, who cares if it is Unferth who bows before the gods returned, or Gormengil? Kill him, or help him. It matters not to me."

Horta was surprised. That she cared nothing for Unferth or Gormengil was irrelevant, but that she had spoken of the gods returning rather than just Char-harash ascending to godhood, that was something that he had not considered. Yet the gods derived their power in no small part from those who worshipped them. If Char-harash was resurrected, if he led armies over the land as he would no doubt do, then the ways of the Kar-ahn-hetep would spread everywhere. And so too their gods. All of them.

"Did you not know?" the goddess whispered from the night. "You seek to raise one god, but with him shall come the others. The old ways are returning. The old battles will be new again."

And then her presence faded and she was gone. Horta continued to contemplate what she had revealed though. It was more, much more than he had anticipated. If the old gods returned, there would be catastrophic war among them as there was of old. It would wreak destruction across all the world. But he had proceeded thus far, and he could not turn back now.

20. Blade and Hilt

Brand was tired, for he had gotten little sleep the night before. But excitement banished his lethargy.

All morning he had watched from the courtyard as new recruits entered the fortress. Often, he spoke with them, or their leaders. He learned where they were from and what part of the Duthgar was home to them. He listened to their changing accents, for even in such a relatively small land there were changes, especially between the eastern and western districts. To the west were other tribes. The Callenor was one, closely associated with the Duthenor through a long history, but there were others.

And it was to his surprise that one group of soldiers, only twenty strong, were from one of these tribes. He heard them talking as they came in, and he knew those accents though he had not heard them since his childhood. They were men of the Norvinor tribe.

They looked skilled warriors. In appearance, they were slightly shorter than the men of the Duthenor usually were, and their hair was black. They wore chain mail that was longer than common, coming down to their knees nearly, and their swords were of a larger kind. They looked grim men, and proud, yet they sang as they marched and there was something jaunty about them despite their appearance. There was curiosity in their eyes too, for they would not have seen a fortress such as this, nor, maybe, even heard the rumors about it.

Brand went over to meet them, and they ceased to sing. Before he could introduce himself, their leader bowed. "Hail, Brand, rightful chieftain of the Duthenor."

Brand was surprised. "You know me?"

The man grinned. "No, but even in our land the legendary Helm of the Duthenor is spoken of in stories. We knew it for what it was the moment we saw you."

Brand wore it so often now that he often forgot it was even there. The man continued. "Bruidiger, I'm called. And I lead these men to your service."

Brand thrust out his hand, and Bruidiger took it in the warrior's grip, wrist to wrist.

"I thank you and your men for your service. But I have to say I'm surprised to see any Norvinor warriors here. You're far from home, and this isn't your battle."

Bruidiger shrugged. "Both of those things are true, and it's only chance that brings us here. We were hired by a merchant to guard his caravan as he came through our lands, and we saw him safely to your own, for he heads through them to Cardoroth. But then we heard what was happening here, and we lingered, intrigued. Then we heard you had returned, and there was friendship once between your father and mine. So I came to help, and my men came to help me."

Brand remembered his father speaking well of the Norvinor, but he had not known he had a friend among them. It was interesting, and he wished to talk to Bruidiger further, but this was not the time nor place.

"If it pleases you, later I'd like to have a good talk. But for now, you and your men must be tired. There'll be a man at the barracks to find you a place to rest and get you a meal. But I'll find you this evening, if I get a chance."

Bruidiger bowed again. Brand signaled one of his own men over, and he led the small band away. He wished he had a thousand more of them, for they had the look of hard warriors about them, men who had seen a fight or two and come out the other side victorious.

155

A little while later another group came through, and this one was several hundred strong. They were from the south of the Duthgar, lands near to the High Way and down into a valley famous for the quality of its cheese. Brand had been there once, and he spoke highly of their home, and they liked that he did. But they gave him sobering news in return. Unferth was close behind them. There would be no more warriors entering the fortress after them.

Brand sent word for all the captains of the army to come out into the courtyard, and there he addressed them when they had gathered.

"Men," he said. "War approaches on swift feet. Soon this fortress will be tested, our strategies probed and the thoroughness of our training examined. But this I know. The fortress is strong, and the hearts of those who defend it beat with courage."

Some of the men cheered. Some looked scared. But most tried to show nothing of what they felt, either way.

"But will we win?" called out one of the captains.

Brand wished he was better at delivering speeches. He always seemed to get this question, but he did not mind. And as always, he gave a truthful answer. Men who risked their lives deserved it.

"I think that we will, else I'd not have come here. But there are no guarantees in life. Victory is not assured. Not for us, but neither is it for Unferth. It will be earned, and the payment will be dealt out in blood and death. That is the truth." He paused, before going on. "And this also is the truth. We have no choice. A fight is coming, and men will die. I could have led Unferth a merry chase around the Duthgar. But I've chosen this place to make a stand. And I stand with you, ready to pay the same price of blood or death that you all are. But if there are any who have changed their minds, I give you leave to go now, freely

156

and without hinderance. I'll have no man here against his will."

He normally offered soldiers a choice like that. It was fair, and it was true too. Better to have only warriors who believed in the cause and a chance of winning. But it was a double-edged sword. If too many took him up on the offer, morale would plummet.

There was silence. No one moved. That too was normal, but he knew by offering them the chance to leave he played on their pride and they were more likely to stay. He was a general, and it was his job to think like that, but he did not like it.

He spoke again to the men, this time infusing his voice with greater passion. He was no speechmaker, but he knew this was the time to rally them to a state of excitement. He had told them death was possible. He had given them the chance to leave. But they were still here, and this was now the time to offer them hope and heat their blood.

"This army started small. It was just a band of a few men. Back then, I called us the point of a sword. But I said it would grow, and it has. Now we have the blade, and edges, and a hilt and pommel. Now, we are complete. Now, we will smite Unferth and free the Duthgar!"

The captains cheered. All of them this time. But Brand could not help wonder how many would die soon. They were a sword in themselves, but Unferth had his own sword. The walls of the fortress would run with blood, and he had made them feel good about it. And he would do worse, yet.

"Captains!" he cried out into the noise, and it subsided. "Tell your men what I have told you. Tell them victory is at hand. The sooner Unferth arrives, the sooner will that victory come!"

The captains cheered again, and then they went back to the barracks talking boisterously. A small group remained, and he saw that this was made up of his friends. Taingern and Shorty glanced at him, and he read approval in their looks. He had done what was necessary. Tinwellen scrutinized him as though she was assessing the value of a gold ring. He did not care much for that gaze, but then she smiled at him and his heart lightened.

But it was Sighern's gaze that troubled him. The boy looked at him with dark eyes. There was almost hostility there.

21. Duels are for the Reckless

The next day dawned to a gray day. Fog marched down the ridges near the fortress, veiling the pine-clad slopes that Brand liked. There were no green trees to be seen, nor a blue sky. And though Brand loved mists and fog and rain also, he did not like this concealing blanket.

As the morning passed, the fogs thinned and drifted away. Yet the sky remained dull and overcast. Rain was coming, and perhaps a storm with it. The air was heavy and oppressive.

But with the parting of the fog came another sight, and it was not the marching of pines up steep-sided ridges that drew his eye, but the marching of soldiers. Unferth had arrived, and his army with him. And though Brand searched among the masses for sign of Horta, he was not visible. Yet still Brand knew he was there. The fog was of his making. It reeked of sorcery and had worked to conceal the coming of the enemy.

Unferth may have thought it a good thing to approach so. But it made no difference. Everyone in the fortress knew they were coming. The last men to join Brand's army had brought word, and his own scouts had been watching them for some time.

Brand stood atop the battlement, the gate tower just to his left. From it the Dragon Banner of the Duthenor hung limply. But that it was present at all would anger Unferth. He would have no liking for what it represented, and its very existence reminded one and all that he had usurped the rule of the Duthgar.

From where he waited, Brand had a clear view of all that transpired, but he kept his eye also on the men lining the ramparts all around. They were quiet and grim, but he saw no panic there. Nor should there be. Unferth's army was bigger, but the men here had grown used to the walls and their advantages. They had discovered by their own training how vulnerable an attacker was who sought to scale it.

Unferth came into sight. He was too far away to recognize by his features, and Brand had last seen him a long, long time ago. But there was no mistaking the armor he wore, for in its way it was as famed as the sword Brand himself carried and the Helm of the Duthenor on his own head.

The helm and armor of Unferth gleamed red as blood, and a shiver went up his spine. Then he smiled to himself. That, of course, was the intention of the color. It could as easily be black, or green or some other hue. But it was red to produce fear in the enemy, to remind them that they might bleed. It also served to highlight the wearer so that his men knew where he was at all times. That could be both a good and a bad thing. Much depended on the leader.

Unferth would be tested here. Would he lead from the front? Would he fight with his men and prove his courage to the warriors he led? If he did, he might die. If he did not, they would not so willingly follow him. It was a hard choice, and one that Brand had made many times. He did not think Unferth had ever been in that position. He was rumored to be a skilled fighter, but he had been involved in skirmishes only and never a war.

Brand knew he would fight. It was his way, but also circumstances dictated it. Unferth was in a more difficult position. The risk of scaling the battlement was great, and retreat was difficult. Not so atop the walls. Brand could fight up here himself, and then step back to let men take his place. All battles were fought in the mind as well as with weapons. Unferth's red armor was a tactic. Brand fighting himself was another. No one could expect a besieging general to scale the walls, but when the enemy leader fought with his own men it would make Unferth look the worse for not doing so.

Even as Brand watched, Unferth came forward out of his host with a small group of men. The warrior beside him held high on a pole the banner of the chieftains of the Callenor. The cloth was snowy white, and upon it was the image of the black talon of a raven.

The Raven Banner infuriated Brand. Who was this man who dared bring it here to Duthenor lands? But that it angered him also worried him. He must be above that. A general must not succumb to such things, but rather be cool and level-headed at all times.

Unferth would not be expected to come to battle without his banner. But that went two ways. Brand gestured to Sighern. "Retrieve our own banner and bring it here, close to me."

The young man moved away and Shorty grunted. "It seems that Unferth wants to parley. And what's going on with his armor? It looks like he's been rolling around in raspberries."

"So it does. But legend says it's dwarven-made. The color is unusual, but it's not lacking in quality. Nor his helm or axe."

"I think it's cute," Tinwellen offered.

Brand had to laugh at that. "Please tell him so when he gets here. No words could be more insulting to him."

"But you'll try to find some anyway?" Taingern asked.

"Of course. If I can upset him, he'll be more likely to make a mistake."

They did not have to wait much longer. Sighern returned, holding aloft the Dragon Banner even as the Raven Banner drew close below and Unferth stood before the wall.

Brand did not wait for the other man to speak. "Hail, Unferth, chieftain of the Callenor, usurper of the Duthgar and murderer. State your business."

The cold voice of Unferth came in reply. If the greeting had bothered him, he gave no sign of it.

"Hail, Brand, outlaw and bandit. You know my business here. It is to bring you to justice for crimes against the Duthgar. You have brought unruly war to the land, and you will be punished."

Brand slowly drew his Halathrin-wrought blade. "By this sword, and the helm I wear, and most of all by the name you have given me, I declare myself the rightful heir to the chieftainship of the Duthenor. Do you deny who I am, or my rights and responsibilities?"

"I deny nothing. I recognize your heritage, and for the proud lineage that is yours I will not hang you as a common criminal. But I am king here now, and your heritage is of no matter. Come down and surrender, and I will show you mercy. Fight, and I will see every man here dead. Either by sword in battle, or hanged as criminals if they surrender too late."

Brand could hardly believe it. Unferth was an idiot. It went against all the stratagems of war to suggest that surrendered soldiers would still be executed. It meant that once the fight began, there was only one way to live, and that was through victory. Without surrender as an option, his army would fight harder, and to the very last. Men with their backs to the wall were the hardest opponent of all to beat.

"You will have to take this fortress first, Unferth, to make good your threat. And that you cannot do."

162

A silence settled between them, cold as ice. But Brand was not done. He spoke into it, his voice even colder and thick with contempt.

"And you name yourself a king? Nay. You are no king. I once served a true king, and you are not his equal. You are a fool wearing a crown of straw."

Even as he spoke, Tinwellen whispered into his ear. "Don't go too far, Brand. There's a chance to make peace here, or he wouldn't have come to speak with you. Thousands will die for your pride if you don't make the attempt."

The weight of her words carried force. There was a truth to them that he could not deny, yet at the same time he felt the futility of it all. War was inevitable, because Unferth would never renounce his rule of the Duthgar, and he himself could not let the murder of his parents go unavenged.

But even so, he heeded Tinwellen, though it was not in the way she intended.

"Unferth!" he called. "At heart, this battle is between us, and us alone. Men will die here, by their hundreds or even thousands. But you and I can stop that. I will come down and fight you, man to man. Let that be an end to our hostility. Let that decide who rules the Duthgar."

Unferth did not answer at once, and the longer he waited the better pleased Brand was. His opponent had not dismissed the challenge out of hand, and the longer he delayed answer the more credence it had. Those who followed him would know he had considered the matter before saying no, if he did so, and they would wonder if it was a lack of courage that informed his decision rather than strategy.

At length, the usurper gave reply. "I am a king, Brand. Duels are for the reckless. I do not gamble the fate of my realm on a battle between two men. Surrender, and I will spare your supports. Fight, and I will kill you all. Choose!"

Sighern shook the Dragon Banner, and he hissed in Brand's ear. "The men who follow you won't ever surrender. They don't just fight for you, but for their own freedom. Send Unferth to hell, and his army with him."

Tinwellen looked at the young man, fury in her eyes. He returned her gaze with cold contempt.

Brand was about to answer Unferth when Hruidgar also whispered into his ear. The hunter had been the last scout to return into the fortress and give Brand news of the approaching enemy.

"Patience, Brand. Stall for time. No more Duthenor can enter the fortress, but that doesn't mean a small army isn't gathering somewhere behind Unferth. Stall, and let time work to your favor. If that happens, we can crush him."

Seldom in his life had Brand ever been indecisive. It seemed to him that all the advice given to him was good, and yet it was all contradictory. How was he to decide?

"Well?" Unferth called up. "What's it to be?"

Brand sheathed his sword, and then leaned forward over the rampart to answer.

"Attack if you dare, Unferth. You'll spill the blood of your men in vain."

The usurper did not seem displeased. "You are proud now, Brand. But when every last one of your men lies dead around you as proof of your folly, I will have you brought to me alive. And then you will kneel at my feet and name me lord. Only then, when you have drunk deep of the dregs of woe, shall I kill you."

Unferth swung away, and he departed with the men he had brought. The Raven Banner hung limply in the oppressive air, and the threat he had voiced hung in it also,

more ominous even than the banner of an enemy nation
in the Duthgar.

22. Battle and Blood

Brand watched silently as the enemy made ready, nor did anyone else speak.

Unferth's army had come prepared. The front ranks moved forward, burdened by hundreds of coiled ropes with grappling hooks tied to their ends. Ladders had been made also. These, as with all the equipment, had a makeshift appearance. All would have been made hurriedly by men who had not observed such equipment in use. None of the Duthenor or Callenor had attacked a fortress before. Not that they were inferior warriors, just that their lords built no fortresses. They were a small people, Duthenor and Callenor alike, and they had no need of fortified strongholds. That might change after this.

The enemy drew closer, plainly visible now. The last trailers of fog had gone. Brand watched them closely, assessing their discipline and how they were organized and how quickly they responded to orders. What he saw was what he expected. They were no match for a professional army of full-time soldiers, but they were not that far behind. The same could be said of his own force, only he had begun to train them well and they had an edge.

Unferth's numbers were more worrisome. Five thousand men marched beneath the shadow of the Raven Banner. It was not a king's army – it was a chieftain's army. Even so, it outnumbered his. Five thousand were set against three. The walls helped there, and Unferth was not the general Brand knew that he was himself. But though the fortress helped in many ways, in that respect it was a partial hindrance. Out in the field Brand's superior skill and experience would show. But the walls reduced tactical choices, and that stole some of his advantage. No matter. War was like that. It took and it gave, it surprised and it ran to expected courses. It was set in its ways and fickle. It was a gamble, and the commander who gambled least had the most chance of winning.

It became clear that Unferth intended a frontal assault. He was not going to try to surround the entire fortress and attack it all at once. Rather, he was going to concentrate on the wall that housed the gate. This was the weakest point, and the tactic made some sense. Other commanders may have acted differently, but Brand did not mind. He was prepared for such eventualities, and every tactic had advantages and disadvantages. This, he considered, worked to his advantage. Unferth felt the gate to be a weakness, but Brand knew it was well repaired and highly protected. The enemy would discover so to their cost.

Horns sounded. Signals were given. A mass of the enemy separated from the main host and began to march forward. As they closed on the fortress, they gathered pace. Finally, they ran with their shields above their heads to protect themselves from the rain of death they feared would come from above.

And that rain fell. Arrows were shot first, the hiss of them as they thickened the air was loud and frightening. Nor could men run, hold up a shield and also carry ladders and ropes well. Especially without training and practice. Arrows struck home, finding gaps and weaknesses. Men died, falling to the ground to lie still. Others jerked and spasmed. All were trampled by those who followed.

Then fell the javelins. These killed fewer, but still wounded many. Again, the wounded were trampled,

167

though some managed to turn their backs to flee. Arrows killed many of these also.

The survivors reached the wall. Faces were visible now. Men with frightened eyes looked up. The wall seemed tall to them, the chances of reaching the top meagre. And when they did, swords still awaited them. Surely, there was no harder task in warfare than what they faced now, and the knowledge of it must have been bitter. So too their curses for Unferth, who had brought them to this.

But the men were brave. Callenor tribesmen may have been the enemy, but Brand admired their courage. They cast up their grappling hooks and pressed their ladders against the wall, and they scrambled up. Speed meant less time to be shot at. Reaching the top of the wall meant a chance to fight, sword to sword and man to man. And if enough of them did so, they might win the rampart and live. So they came on, desperately.

They were met with dropped rocks, many the size of a man's head. Helms were little defense against this. Shields offered better protection, but it was awkward to hold one and climb at the same time. Even doing so, many men were dislodged to plummet, screaming, to death below.

And yet the enemy came on, driven by a need to reach the top for a chance at survival and supported by their large numbers. It seemed that their attempts to do so were futile, but those who lived climbed with speed and those above who cast missiles must make space for the men who hacked away at scaling ropes and dislodged ladders with poles.

Brand watched, hearing the sounds of battle that he hated, seeing men's heads cracked open like melons or bodies broken in death below. He felt triumph at the difficulty the enemy had in even reaching their opponent, and he felt gut-wrenchingly sick at the terrible deaths meted out. He watched, and he heard, and he wished it to keep going and to stop all at once. It was war, and he had done this before, and if he lived, must needs likely do it again.

A warrior hacked away at the rope that held a grappling hook nearby. He used a large knife, and severed the fibers quickly. Men fell screaming below, and their deaths were a costly error on Unferth's head. The ropes had not been twined with wire at the end to make the severing more difficult.

Quickly the warrior bent and picked up the metal grappling hook. For a moment it looked as though he was about to cast it down at the enemy, and then he remembered his training. Instead, he threw it to the rear of the battlement. It was one grappling hook the enemy would not have for their next attack. It was metal that could be repurposed into arrow and spear heads.

But despite the appalling slaughter, the weight of numbers and desperation of the enemy carried through. They began to reach the top, and the clash of sword against sword rang in the air. This gave encouragement to those below, and they swarmed up in a wave.

The enemy surged through the crenels first, where the gap in the battlement allowed archers to shoot. Then they clambered over the merlons next, which gave protection to the archers. This was the more dangerous, for from that greater height they could leap into the defenders, and this they did with swinging swords and wild cries.

Most died. The swords of the defenders flashed in answer. Their own battle cries rose up. But in killing these men others were given opportunity to clear the wall and fight man to man.

A warrior thrust his sword at Brand. With a neat twist of his own blade, Brand deflected the point and sent a riposte back that tore away the warrior's throat. Sighern knocked the blade from the warrior's now weak grip and

169

thrust him back against the battlement. A moment he staggered there, blood coursing from his throat, and then Sighern toppled him over the edge. He screamed, blood spraying from his mouth. A thump and more screams followed as he dislodged other attackers from rope or ladder.

To Brand's left, another warrior broke through, but Tinwellen was there before him, a knife in each hand and both flashing. The man died before her swift onslaught, and she pulled a bloody knife from the eye-slit of his helm and kicked him away.

All over the battlement the same was happening. If the enemy broke through a little more, the battle would be won. If Brand's men kept them at bay, the numbers of those climbing must diminish, and the defenders would hold. It hung in the balance, and Brand fought with a cold fire in his belly. More attackers came over the wall, more died at his hand and the hands of others.

There was a momentary lull. No new grappling hooks were thrown up, at least not where Brand stood near the gate, and he leaned through a crenel to look out at the enemy. They still came up the wall like spiders. In the distance, Unferth stood out in his red armor, arms waving and seeming to bellow instructions. He was sending a new wave of attackers.

The lull did not last long. In moments more warriors confronted Brand. They swarmed over the ramparts, screaming and slashing with their swords. Brand fought back, his blade cutting gleaming arcs through the air. Blood sprayed his face. Blood slicked the stone beneath his boots and made footing unsteady. On it went, and then out of nowhere a bright light flashed, dazzling his eyes.

He staggered back, killing the enemy who followed him by instinct alone and not by sight, for he could barely see.

Then Char-harash was there, his eyes blazing and a wicked sword flashing for Brand's throat.

Brand weaved to the side, and used his own blade to deflect his enemy's attack, but his blade struck nothing. Too late he realized this was in his mind, that some sorcery had planted the image there. He felt the mind of Char-harash nearby, and his own magic came to life pushing the presence of the sorcerer away.

It took only moments, but the distraction had its effect. Brand's attention had been taken from the real attackers that came for him, and a mighty blow from an axe crashed against the Helm of the Duthenor. Sparks flew into the air, and Brand staggered, dropping his sword.

Death was upon him. But Sighern was there, his sword killing the axe-man, and then Shorty and Taingern came to his side, their blades flashing and their eyes burning with a cold light. The enemy was repelled, but Brand felt his knees give way and he tumbled to the ground beside his sword. Darkness swamped him, and he knew no more.

His mind swam through the blackness, and everything was vague and unformed. Then slowly it seemed that he rose up. There was light again, and he knew who he was and where. His eyes flickered open.

He was not sure how much time had passed. Moments? Hours? It did not feel like it had been a great length of time. He was on the ground, his head in Tinwellen's lap. She was caressing his face. Nearby was Sighern, a bloodied cloth at his neck, wet with blood. He had killed the axe-man, but not without cost. The axe-man must have returned a near killing blow before he died.

Brand was not sure if he had not seen these things after the blow to his head, or if he just could not remember. And the dull throbbing in his head did not help, nor the sharp pain in his neck where muscles and tissues must have been torn or twisted by the mighty blow.

171

The Helm of the Duthenor lay nearby. It was unmarked and undented. The Halathrin wrought things well, with the skills immortality and magic lent them. It had saved his life.

A great cheer went up along the ramparts, and Brand tried to stand. A roaring pain filled his head and he fell back down, Tinwellen cradling him.

"What's happening?" he asked.

Taingern seemed to come from nowhere, and he knelt down with concern showing in his eyes.

"We've repulsed the enemy. And we don't think they'll come again today. They had thought to take us in one great rush, but that failed, and they've learned what it's like to attack a fortress. No, they'll not come again today. Their losses are great in equipment, men and morale. Unferth must be chewing his own tongue right about now."

Brand wanted to answer, but the blackness was coming up to swamp him again.

23. Gormengil

Night fell, but the mood of the camp had long since been dark. Men muttered under their breaths. Treason was in the air. Not just of Gormengil, but in the heart of every warrior. Unferth had been confident of swift victory. He had promised it. But the attack had been a slaughter.

Horta could not say he was overly surprised. Always Brand did the unexpected, but never anything without reason. If he chose to fight behind walls, he did so because it gave him an advantage. His every move was dangerous, but Su-sarat should have him in thrall by now. Or perhaps he was even dead. Men had claimed he had been struck a killing blow by an axe.

Warriors eyed Horta coldly as he walked through the camp. Unferth had summoned him, and the messenger looked frightened. Everyone looked frightened. There was a dangerous feel to the air, and a sense that the world was shifting. So be it. But Unferth was right to call another war council. He would have to be open to ideas now, and a new plan would be developed. They still had the greater number of soldiers, and the enemy must fall, especially with a better-planned attack.

He came to Unferth's tent, but tonight a fire was set before it and the king's men sat outside. He was the last to reach it, and the others had been waiting.

A thin drizzle of rain began to fall. It had been coming and going these last few hours, but still the stars could be seen at whiles through breaks in the scudding clouds. But his knee ached, and he knew heavier rain was approaching.

Horta took a place near the fire, turning his knee toward the heat. No one greeted him, and he offered none himself. Only Gormengil glanced at him, his eyes as unreadable as ever. But the man looked away swiftly, and Horta felt the stirrings of unease. At that moment, Unferth pulled aside the tent flap and exited his tent. He remained dressed in full armor, and the raven axe was in his hand. He intended to remind people of his authority tonight. It would not be pleasant.

Unferth did not take a seat. He stood to address them. "We gave Brand a bloody nose today. It may even be that he is dead. But tomorrow, we will take the fortress. Even as we speak, men are working, and will continue to work through the night, to make new grappling ropes and ladders. Tomorrow, the enemy will fall. Count on it."

It was a confident speech. But he had spoken like that before. Horta glanced around him, assessing the mood of the men. Had Unferth done the same, he would not have spoken as he had. The men were in no mood for false confidence and bravado. Too many had died today, and too greatly had they underestimated Brand and overestimated their ability to take a fortress. Unferth was responsible for that, only he was not accepting it. Where he should have been asking for advice, he was saying the same things he had been for days, and his men knew it for incompetence now.

No one answered him. Even Gormengil remained silent, staring at the ground as though no sight was more interesting.

"Well?" Unferth said. "Does no one here have a voice? I expect enthusiasm from those I lead. And I expect them to impart that same confidence to the army. That's your job as leaders."

"We were beaten today," Gormengil answered. He had raised his gaze from the dirt and there was shame in his eyes. "We were beaten, and we should not have been. Had we—"

"Enough!" roared Unferth. "I expect better from you. I expect better from all my captains. You must learn to be resilient. What use are you if you fall apart at the slightest setback?"

Horta could see that Gormengil struggled to maintain his mask of detachment. Emotions chased themselves over his face. Anger, resentment, disbelief and then finally determination.

"The fault is not ours," he said softly. "Almost, we had the enemy. Almost. But they rallied. Brand fought on the wall, and his men fought with him. But you? You stayed back from the bloodshed. Had you gone forward in the battle and given encouragement, had you climbed the wall yourself we would have overrun them. But you did not see the moment that you should have done so. Or you did, and you were too cowardly to act."

Unferth went pale. "You dare to—"

"I dare because it's true." Gormengil spoke in a steady voice, void of emotion.

The king gripped the haft of his axe tightly. "You're dismissed, Gormengil. Not just from this meeting. Leave. Flee! I exile you from the realm, and your life is forfeit if ever I see you again."

Gormengil slowly shook his head. "I don't think so. You're not fit to lead us. You're a coward and incompetent. I challenge you under our ancient laws. It is my right, as heir."

"You're no longer heir!"

"I am, and I challenge you to a fight, as the law permits, for the leadership of the Callenor tribe."

Horta studied the men gathered there, and he saw that Unferth did also. No one met his gaze. They would not intervene, for they saw Gormengil as someone who might

175

lead them to victory and Unferth as someone who had led them to disaster.

It was for this reason that Horta had hurried after the king, to stop such a challenge. He *must* stop it, or at least he had thought so. But now? Now, he felt the dragon's breath blow across the land. Destiny was in the air. He would not intervene.

Unferth grunted in disgust. He must know that he had lost the support of the men, but he knew also that if he killed Gormengil he would remove any real alternative to leadership. And the armor of his forefathers gave him confidence. As well it might. Horta sensed the magic in it, though it was of a kind unfamiliar to him. And though Unferth had a tendency to cowardice, he now had his back to the wall. He would fight, and he might well win.

"Come and die then, boy," Unferth said. He moved away a little from the men to give himself room to move. He would need it, for wicked as the axe looked it was an unwieldy weapon.

Gormengil joined him. His sword hissed from his scabbard, and the cold gaze of his eyes was even more remote than normal. A block of ice gave off more emotion.

But Horta knew it was there. And often those who showed the least emotion were those who felt it the strongest.

Unferth struck first. The raven-axe flew through the air, and it whistled as it did so by some art of its makers. It was a lightning strike, and Horta was confounded. How had Unferth moved so quickly?

Gormengil darted nimbly to the side, but even so, he only barely avoided one of the blades of the axe that would have severed his head from his body in a single stroke.

If the whistling of the axe surprised him, he did not show it. Perhaps the Callenor knew that as one of its properties.

The king kept moving. His first stroke had missed, and now he was vulnerable because the weight of the axe meant it could not be returned to a guard position nor could a follow-up blow be delivered quickly. Yet Unferth surprised Horta again.

Either by great strength or a lightness to the axe that Horta could hardly credit, the blades twisted in midflight and swept back in a reverse cut.

For all his speed and nimbleness, Gormengil was caught out. He was moving in to drive his own blade forward in a killing thrust when the axe bore down on him again.

There was no time to retreat. The axe was angling downward, so he could not duck. Instead, he jerked his blade toward the axe where the head met the haft. There it caught it, deflecting the blow but not stopping it.

One of the blades of the axe sliced down into the heir's side. Gormengil staggered away, fortunate to only receive a glancing blow. Yet still his chain mail vest was rent there, frayed as easily as rope by a knife.

Even so, Gormengil showed nothing of the pain or emotion he felt. He was like a wall of stone, immoveable, and Horta admired him for it. Unferth, however, grinned, and he swung the axe leisurely before him in slow circles.

"Your pride has killed you," the king taunted. "You're no match for me."

Gormengil did not answer. He merely gazed at his opponent with dark eyes, and his lack of fear or reaction seemed to enrage Unferth. The king leapt forward again, his axe hurtling, and this time it did not whistle but moaned. It was an underhanded cut, unexpected and swift.

But Gormengil seemed to have anticipated it, for he stepped a little to the side with time to spare and his sword crashed into the dwarven helm.

This time, it was the king who staggered back. Gormengil was upon him, his blade flashing in cuts and thrusts quicker than the eye could follow. Three times Unferth would have died save for the quality of armor he wore, but Gormengil made one strike too many and overbalanced slightly in his haste. Unferth saw his opportunity and the raven-axe moaned again, this time thrust forward so that the spike at the head of the blades could pierce armor and then hook out entrails.

The heir to the throne dived and rolled. He avoided the thrust but a follow-up slash caught him a glancing blow to his helmet. But this time he did not retreat. He stepped in close, avoiding the sweeping danger of the axe and drove a knife deep into the king's thigh, then leapt back, the blood-wetted knife in one hand and his sword in the other.

Unferth screamed. It was not a fatal wound, but he would weaken swiftly and lose strength in his legs if it was not bandaged. The raven-axe flew once more, whistling even as Unferth screamed, and it cut the air like a streaking shadow.

But this time Gormengil was quicker. Perhaps he had held back before. Or perhaps the sight of Unferth's blood gave him hope of victory and purpose. Either way he stepped in to meet the attack. The axe whistled, but Gormengil's sword sliced, and it severed the king's hand in one blow above the black gauntlet.

The axe thudded to the ground. Unferth's severed hand fell silently, looking out of place on the grass. Blood spurted from the stump, and the king, wide-eyed, looked in shock at his own gauntleted hand as it lay before him.

Unferth fell to his knees. He screamed again, a terrible sound to hear, but Gormengil was deaf to it. Slowly, step by step he approached, his sword steady before him.

The heir to the throne, he who now would rule, struck swiftly at his uncle. His blade flashed, cutting between the bottom of the helm and the top of the chain mail coat, and it found the small gap there.

Unferth toppled over and stopped screaming, but Horta was not sure if he was dead. Gormengil reached down though, one hand dislodging the helm and with the blade in the other he began to hack.

After some moments, he held up the head of Unferth. "He was a fool, and look where it got him?" He cast the head aside. "I am not a fool. I will lead you better."

No one said anything. The men were stunned, but Horta knew instinctively what to do and acted quickly. He stepped over to the fallen raven-axe and picked it up. He marveled at the feel of it in his hands and the lightness of it. Of what metal the blades were made, he did not know. Yet still he felt the deadliness of the weapon. Nor could he see any nick or blemish on the metal, which there should have been.

He approached Gormengil. "Hail, Gormengil, king by blood, and by right, and by victory in battle. Take your axe, and if you will have it, my service also." He bowed slightly, and lifted up the weapon.

Gormengil wrapped a hand around the axe haft, and Horta saw his eyes widen a fraction when he took it. He, too, marveled at the lightness of it.

"Truly," Gormengil muttered. "It is a weapon of magic." His gaze fell on Horta, and his eyes were emotionless again. "I will accept your service." There may have been no emotion there, but there *was* a glint of knowledge. He understood that Horta had just set the tone of how to react, and Unferth's counselors all approached. One by one they knelt and swore their oaths of loyalty.

When they were done, Gormengil spoke. "Go forth among the men. Tell them that the Callenor have a new chieftain, and this one is not so craven as not to fight himself." Then he hefted the axe wickedly through the air, making it whistle and moan.

24. Two Battles

Brand woke. It was dark, save for the wavery light of a single candle. There was a roaring in his head, and a dull ache, but a soft hand touched his forehead, and Tinwellen's voice came to him, suddenly clear above the roaring. "Sleep," she commanded. And Brand slept.

When he woke again, the light of the candle was gone and the gray of dawn filled the room he had in the barracks. Of Tinwellen, there was no sign, but Shorty and Taingern were there, their faces grim.

"What news?" Brand asked.

"First," Taingern said, "how do you feel?"

Brand was not sure. The roaring in his head had lessened, but not gone. And the dull ache had receded, but not entirely. And there was a stiffness in his shoulder and neck that troubled him.

"Given that I could be dead, I feel well enough."

Shorty grunted. "Make light of it if you will, but it was a bad blow you took. Or that the Helm of the Duthenor took. A crown it might be to the Duthenor, but the skill of the Halathrin who made it saved your life."

Brand knew that was true. But his two friends had not come here to tell him so. Something had happened, otherwise at least one of them would be on the battlements.

A look passed between the two of them, and he knew they judged him well enough to hear it, whatever it was.

"There's good news … and strange news," Taingern said. "First, and obviously, we repulsed the enemy yesterday. They did not attack again."

Brand nodded, and wished he had not. A wave of dizziness rolled over him.

"And the strange news?"

"Well, that's possibly tied to the first. Their losses were heavy yesterday, and it seems that Unferth paid the price for it. Just now, as it began to grow light, we saw the enemy had put his head on a pole just before the gate. Obviously, they have a new leader."

Brand was shocked. All his life it seemed had been wrapped up in the idea of deposing Unferth and avenging his parents. And now … the man was dead. It seemed that he no longer had direction or purpose. But there was an element of relief too. Vengeance was a heavy burden.

He closed his eyes and thought briefly of his parents. Justice had been done at last, and though it was not by his hand, it did not matter. It *was* because of him though, because if he had not pressed Unferth and made him suffer military losses, the usurper would not have been deposed. More importantly, whatever he had done in the past, whatever he did now, it was for the benefit of the Duthgar. That was the one thing that must guide him.

Brand opened his eyes. "Do we know who leads the enemy now?"

Shorty shook his head. "We know Unferth had an heir. The men say he's called Gormengil, and he's Unferth's nephew. Whether he's now in charge though, we don't know. But the enemy has certainly not left."

Brand considered that. A new leader could change everything, but it probably would not. Whoever had deposed Unferth was not likely to free the Duthgar and return to Callenor lands.

But whatever happened, he was needed now on the ramparts.

"Help me up, lads. I'm a bit wobbly."

They looked at him carefully but did not argue. Not even when he had to lean on them just to stand. But after a little while the roaring in his head subsided again and the dizziness passed. Mostly. He left the room on his own two feet, but Shorty and Taingern stayed close, lest he fall.

Dawn broke silently over the ancient fortress, and color leached through the gray remnants of night. But the air was oppressive with the threat of imminent rain, and no sound could be heard in all the vastness of armed men. This would be another day of death, and the start of it was right before them.

Brand had been ready for it, but still the shock of seeing a head on a pole near the gate was sobering. That it was Unferth's … was, in some way, worse.

Even in death the Usurper looked at him, somehow seeming to accuse him personally for such a horrible fate. And Brand felt sorry for him, and wondered that that was possible.

A lone horn blew, sending a wail up into the gray-clad sky. As though awaiting that signal, a horseman cantered forward from the enemy camp. He came to stop before the gate, and there he looked up at Brand. The head of Unferth close to his own.

"In the name of the new Lord of the Duthenor and Callenor tribes, I command you to open the gate and surrender. If you do so, Gormengil will let you live. If you do not, you will die. Unless you surrender during battle. Those are his terms, and no other. You have one hour."

The messenger did not look at Unferth's head. He gave no sign of what he thought of the fate of his old lord nor the prospects of the new. Neither did he wait for a reply. Skillfully, he eased his horse backward a few steps, his eyes locked on Brand's, and then he turned and cantered back to the enemy host.

"Not as talkative as Unferth was," Shorty commented.

"And yet an eloquent message all the same," Brand said. "And this time a better strategy behind it. The threat of death is balanced by the offer of life."

They did not discuss what action to take. For Brand, there was nothing to do but fight. Unferth had usurped the rule of the Duthgar, and Gormengil now the same. Nor was there sign any that the defenders felt differently. They wanted freedom from Callenor rule. They had fought for it. Some had died for it. And those who lived were committed to the same course, unwaveringly and with courage.

The hour passed quietly. The threat of rain deepened, and it grew darker instead of lighter as the day wore on. But at the end of the hour, movement rippled through the enemy host. A bonfire sprang to life, flames twisting high into the air, and many horns sounded all at once.

Brand recognized Horta near the bonfire. And there were others with him, dressed in the same type of strange garb that the magician wore. Slowly, Horta leading them, they began to circle the fire. Brand was not familiar with their rites, but he understood the purpose well enough. Horta would invoke some form of sorcery.

But at the same time the warriors of the enemy began to attack. Many were held in reserve, but a great wave of them, greater even than yesterday, rushed forward. They were better prepared for the onslaught that greeted them. Arrows thickened the air, and many fell. But they held their shields better this time, and fewer were killed. The same happened when the javelins were thrown. Men died, but not so many, nor enough. Yesterday, they had gained the top of the rampart with less men. Today, they would do so again, and the danger was greater.

But the defenders now had greater confidence. They knew what they were about. They would not be broken easily, and they knew the task of the enemy was harder and more dangerous than their own. They had learned the wall was their friend, and how to utilize it better to their advantage. And they had won the battle yesterday. No matter how hard things would soon become, that knowledge would buoy them.

Onward the enemy came, and the slaughter was terrible. But they gained the rampart and steel struck steel as blades flashed.

Tinwellen stayed near Brand, and Sighern also. Neither fought, for they acted as his guards. Dizziness had not left him, and the roaring in his head seemed to rise to match the tumult of battle. But he held his sword in his hand, ready to fight as best he could, if he must.

Shorty and Taingern were among the battling warriors. Even as they were of different temperaments, so too were their fighting styles unalike. Yet men fell dead where they went, and the enemy melted away before them.

Brand watched the ebb and flow of battle, trying to remain detached as a general must. But this was sometimes easier done fighting than watching. Too many times he saw men plummet screaming from the battlement. Too often he watched as a man's sword hand was hacked away, or his entrails spilled. Blood sprayed through the air, gore slicked the stone of the rampart, and the moaning and screaming was louder than the constant roaring in his ears.

It could not go on long as things were. One side or the other must gain ascendancy. And Brand sensed a change. The enemy were excited. Soon he saw why. Up over the rampart climbed a red-armored figure. Gormengil himself, and in one hand he held the legendary raven-axe of the Callenor.

This was the moment. The battle would turn one way or the other now. Brand must fight him, and on the outcome of that fight the greater fight would depend.

But even as he took a step forward, he saw the dead enemy on the blood-slicked stone begin to jerk. Dead hands grabbed once more for sword hilts. Dead throats screamed a war-cry in a language that no Callenor tribesman had ever spoken.

Horta had unleashed some foul sorcery, and Brand must combat it. The defenders would not long stand if those they killed rose from the floor and slew them in turn.

But he could not fight Gormengil and counter Horta at the same time. But which could he ignore? The answer froze him to the spot. To ignore either was to lose the battle, and swiftly.

25. The Prophecy of the Witch

Brand was frozen in doubt. The roaring in his ears rose to a shrieking gale. The world seemed to spin, but he steadied himself. Yet still, he did not move. Some other power had risen also, and he felt the force of it threatening to tumble him into blackness again.

The very air filled with a sense of malice. The hatred was so strong that it turned his stomach. But it was not sorcery of Horta's making. That much he knew instinctively. It had a different feel to it, a feel both distant and yet somehow familiar.

Mist rose from the stone of the rampart. From that vague turning and twining of tendrils figures emerged. They were men. They were warriors, though they looked different from any Brand had ever seen. Their armor was strange. So too their swords. But they had the look of the eagle about them, of warriors who knew how to fight and had endured all that the world, and battle, and life could throw at them.

Even as Brand understood what was happening, the figure of Kurik, wizard-priest of the Letharn appeared before him. The man seemed taller than the warriors he led. He seemed stronger, more life-like. And the sense of malice that came from him was overpowering. His hatred had endured through the eons, and though his true enemies were dead, their descendants yet lived in Horta and his followers.

A moment Brand held the gaze of Kurik. No words passed between them, but the spirit of the dead man seemed to swell and grow. His eyes flashed and then he

187

shot like an arrow of light, arcing over the battlement and toward Horta.

Brand looked around again. All over the battlement the dead Horta had raised were being hacked by the ghost-warriors of the Letharn. The Duthenor had crowded back, pressing themselves against the rear of the rampart, and no harm came to them.

Through the turmoil Brand's gaze met Gormengil's. Hatred burned between them, fierce as the sun. Yet the fray swept between them, and though each was ready to fight the other, desperately wanted to fight the other, it was not fated at that moment.

The press of men around Gormengil drew him back to the rampart, and there, taking hold of ropes and ladders they fled. Few warriors stood up to an onslaught of ghosts, though to Brand's eyes it seemed that the spirits only attacked the sorcerous dead that Horta had raised.

The ghosts of the Letharn faded away as the Callenor retreated. Their spirits were free at last, tied no longer to this world nor the last tragedy that they had endured here. But they had won a final victory for themselves, though Brand knew not for him. The enemy would regroup. They had failed yet again, but they were not defeated. A third time yet they would try to take the fortress.

He moved to the edge of the rampart, and all along the wall the Duthenor did the same. Out over the field the enemy sprinted back to their own host, fearful of what had happened on the wall but still alive. And the crimson figure of Gormengil was among them.

"He runs as fast as his men," Shorty said, his gaze on the same figure.

"But he is a man of pride," Brand answered, "and all the harder will he come against us again when the time comes."

Shorty did not dispute it. Nor anyone else. The army below them was in disarray, but it was not broken. The bonfire was scattered into burning debris across the field, scattered sparks and coils of smoke. Of Horta and his followers, there was no sign. Brand hoped he was dead, but did not think it would be so.

Almost Brand ordered a sortie, and he saw the question in the eyes of Taingern and Shorty. They had both thought of it, but he shook his head. The confusion of the enemy was momentary. The ghosts of the Letharn were gone and Gormengil was alive to regroup his men, and he would do so quickly. And still the enemy outnumbered him.

They watched from the walls, and Brand decided what he had to do.

"Gormengil is the key," he said quietly.

The others looked at him, and Sighern voiced their question. "The key to what?"

"To victory. To saving lives, or trying to. He wants to fight me. I want to fight him. If I kill him, the Callenor will have no true leader left. Gormengil binds them better than Unferth, but without him, they have no one."

"A duel then?" Sighern said.

Tinwellen shook her head. "No. I won't permit it. You're still injured. You can't beat him. You need just a little longer to—"

"It's the right thing to do," Sighern interrupted her. "You must fight him, and you must beat him."

Tinwellen turned her dark gaze on the young man, and her look was cold as death. But then she ignored him and swung back to Brand, placing her hands around his head.

Brand felt the coolness of her touch, and he marveled at the joy she brought him. But the roaring in his ears seemed to rise and swell, and the dizziness that was with him ever since he had been struck in the head weakened his legs. Almost he fell, but not quite. And as though from a great distance he heard Sighern's voice again.

"Let him go, witch!"

Abruptly her touch was gone from him. He opened his eyes and realized Sighern had pushed her away. The cold light in her eyes was bleaker than he had ever seen it, and amazed he watched as two knives appeared as if by magic in her hands and she darted at Sighern.

But Sighern acted quicker than she thought. His sword was still drawn from the battle, and reflexively he lifted it and thrust as she came at him.

Tinwellen drove herself onto the point, and then staggered back. The blade slid out of her belly, and Brand knew it for a mortal wound.

No one moved. Shock gripped them. But instead of falling Tinwellen hissed. And Brand wondered that there was no blood, but at the same time he sensed the presence of magic, of a spell unraveling.

Tinwellen swayed, and her figure blurred. In her hands the knives dissolved into the air and were gone. Her lustrous dark hair grew longer still, but paler. The complexion of her skin darkened. Taller she stood, more queenly, and her eyes were black pits of malevolence.

A moment she stood thus, as surprised as any. But her disguise was gone, the magic that transformed her broken. It was the Trickster of which Kurik had warned him, and had never been Tinwellen at all.

Brand raised his sword and summoned his magic. Before him stood a goddess of the old world, and who knew what powers she commanded.

But she made no move to attack. "Fool! You could have had endless joy. Instead, you will die in a meaningless place in a forgotten land."

"All men die," Brand answered. "Now begone, Trickster. Or we shall see if cold steel can find the colder heart of a goddess."

She gazed at him, seemingly in surprise. "How do you know me? No! Never mind. Now I know. He that led the spirits of the dead told you." She drew herself up, and now she looked like a queen to whom all other queens would bow. "Put away your sword. You will not need it against me. This game is up, and another begins. You will die here soon, and even if you do not, then know the futility of all you do. An army of the Kar-ahn-hetep marches even as we speak. Great warriors are they, and their numbers will overrun the Duthgar. And then the Dark God will rise, and on his conquest of lands and realms the old gods will return from memory to stride the lands that are theirs once more. Die, Brand. Despair, and die!"

So speaking, the goddess raised her hands and the figure that was hers, or one of her many likenesses, turned to pale smoke and then vanished.

Brand lowered his sword and rested his weight upon it. His gaze fell to Sighern. "Once more, it seems, you have proved your worth. Your eyes saw deeper than mine, and I thank you."

Brand wasted no time. Nothing felt right, but it rarely did.

He feared he was not fit for what he intended, but he must do it and he must win. Else the bloodshed would be catastrophic. And he knew one thing more, for he believed what the Trickster said about the army marching toward him, but he dare not think of that. Not yet.

He walked through the gate of the fortress and past the pole topped with Unferth's head, his stride seemingly sure, but he knew how weak his legs were, how close to falling he was, and that the roar in his head continued. He kept

191

his gaze off the head, lest he vomit. Nausea accompanied the roaring.

With him came Sighern. He carried a flag, but it was not the Dragon Banner. Instead, it was a red cloth, the sign of parley in the Duthgar, and a light drizzle fell that dampened it. With him was also Hruidgar the Huntsman. Shorty and Taingern remained inside. They would lead the Duthenor if Brand fell.

They did not ride. They walked in order to be sure nothing they did could be taken as an attack. And, although Brand told no one, he feared he would fall dismounting from a horse.

"Are you sure this is a good idea?" Hruidgar asked. "Do the Callenor even know what the red flag means? Can we trust them?"

"It may not be a good idea," Brand answered. "But it's the best I have. And I don't know what the red flag signifies to them. But the Callenor are men like the Duthenor. They have honor, even if Unferth did not."

Hruidgar gave him a long look, but the man said nothing.

Brand liked him for that, so he offered something more. "Regardless, they know who I am by my helm. They will let us pass through until we reach Gormengil."

"And what then?"

"Then what will be will be."

Ahead of them, the faces of the enemy became clear. They were hard men, and war had treated them harshly. But they said nothing, and offered no word of scorn nor greeting. They simply gazed silently, showing nothing of what they felt, and parted to allow Brand and his small entourage through.

It remained the same as they walked through the heart of the army. Men stared at them, but said nothing. Yet a ripple of movement was always ahead of them, opening a way. Until they reached the center of the camp. Once there, the enemy closed around them again, and it was not a comfortable feeling.

But Brand had found what he sought. Here was a tent, and a makeshift table before it. Men were gathered there, and one of them was Horta. He had wished the man dead, but he was not. Yet still, he seemed haggard and his eyes held a hint of fear. The ghost of Kurik had treated him as harshly as war had treated the Callenor. Brand met his gaze and allowed himself the faintest of smiles. The other man looked away.

There was no more time for such games. One figure, and one figure alone, now drew his gaze and held all his attention. Gormengil stood from where he had sat at the table and faced him. In his hands he held the wicked-looking raven axe. It had two blades, and each was swept back like wings but there was a stabbing spike in the middle, curved slightly to resemble a beak. It could be used to stab, but also to hook and gouge. Brand knew the weapon, or at least some of the legends of the Callenor about it. A shiver of fear ran through him.

The red-lacquered chain mail he wore stood out. Supposedly, it was invincible to blade or dart. Time would soon reveal the truth of those stories. But it was the helm that stood out most of all. This, like the rest, was fashioned by the dwarves, and spells were cast upon it. Engraved into the same red-lacquered metal as the chain mail was a single dwarven rune: karak. Legend said it signified victory in their language. But whose? In a fight, always one lost and the other won. The rune would not change that, nor give the wearer of the helm advantage. Even so, it was an unlucky omen to see borne by an opponent.

Through the grim-looking eye slit of the fabled helm, Gormengil's dark eyes gazed out, cold and implacable.

Brand shivered again. Had he at last met his match? Had he finally risked too much in overconfidence?

Gormengil spoke, his voice cold as his eyes and strangely shaped by the metal of the helm.

"Have you come to offer surrender?"

"Not that. Never that. And why should I when the ghosts of the fortress serve the Duthenor?" It was a lie, but the enemy did not know that.

Gormengil nodded gravely, as though he expected such an answer and approved.

"Then why come at all?"

"To give you what you want."

There was a silence then, deep and undisturbed. Eventually, Gormengil moved, tilting his head slightly to one side.

"I want many things. As many as there are stars in the sky."

Brand laughed, but he was not sure how loud. The laughter and the roaring in his ears seemed one and the same thing.

"Life will teach you, if you live it long enough, that less is more. As it is in all things. But no matter. I have come to give you that which we nearly had on the rampart. I have come to fight you, man to man."

The dark eyes of Gormengil gleamed. "I had feared that fight would not come. Some said you were killed by an axe blow."

"I'm a hard man to kill."

"That I know. But no man lives forever." Gormengil's dark eyes studied him, boring into Brand like a force of nature before he spoke again. "And what terms do you propose?"

"Terms? We have no need of terms. You will not surrender, though I offer you peace if you do. No. We have no need of terms. Let the victor discuss such things with whomever leads his opponents when our fight is done. All I ask as that the men with me be allowed to leave unharmed to return to the fortress."

Gormengil nodded. "That I grant."

They said no more, for no more was needed. Brand drew his Halathrin-wrought blade, and the faint drizzle covered it in an instant sheen of moisture. In the distance, thunder rumbled and a wind picked up, scattering rain-scented dust into the air.

Gormengil adjusted his helm and stepped forward. The axe he carried lightly, and every move he made was one of the true-born warrior. Had Brand been well, he knew he could still kill this man. But he was not well.

A space was cleared for them. Silence fell so deep that Brand thought he could hear his own heart thud in his chest. Or perhaps that was thunder growing closer. He could not tell over the roaring in his ears.

Brand struck first. The quicker he finished this fight, the better. The longer it went on, the worse he would fare.

His blade flashed. Like lightning it shattered the gloomy air, but no thunder followed. A strike that should have hit his enemy's head merely cut air as Gormengil dodged to one side.

"You disappoint me, Brand. I had heard that you were a great warrior. It seems that your legend is nothing more than words."

Brand stood still and fought off a wave of dizziness from his sudden movement. "The blow I took to the head nearly killed me. I'm not at my best."

Let Gormengil make of that what he would. No warrior would admit such a weakness in the middle of a fight. But Brand knew his opponent was good enough to see some of the difficulties he was having. Let him wonder then if what he said was truth, or a ruse.

Gormengil began to circle him warily. The axe was held high, yet not so high as to deter another slash at his head. For that reason Brand made no such blow. Instead, he dropped low and sent a wicked strike at his opponent's knees.

The sword was always going to be quicker than the axe. It was the nature of the weapons, so Gormengil nimbly leapt back. Yet still the axe dropped low to block the blow, and it did so swiftly. From this, Brand learned two things. His opponent was unused to fighting with an axe, else he would have trained his reaction to simply be one of retreat, still holding the axe high and ready to strike. And that the axe was lighter than it looked.

But Gormengil had learned something too. Even as Brand slashed at his legs he had struggled to rise. His legs felt weak, and even when he regained his normal stance he swayed where he stood. Gormengil had learned his weakness was likely not feigned.

The Callenor warrior came at him then, the raven-axe flying through the air. It moaned and whistled strangely. Brand paid that no heed. He had expected it. He had *not* expected the speed and power of his opponent though.

Gormengil fell upon him like a toppling mountain. Brand dodged and weaved, using his feet to move away rather than blocking with his sword. Swords did not block axes, yet still he should have had time to see a gap and strike back. Yet no such opportunity came.

Gormengil wove the axe through the air in deadly arcs, but they were tight and narrow. Where the weight of the weapon should have slowed him at the end of a slash and made it hard to change direction and send back a reverse cut, it did not.

Brand saw no opening to attack. Instead, he was forced to strike at Gormengil's gauntleted hands in the hope of injuring him. This was a lesser tactic, for no death blow could be delivered that way.

Gormengil stayed his attack, and grinned at Brand. "Not easy, is it? I found a way to defeat Unferth, though. But now I know I'm better than you. Better than the fabled—"

The axe was light, but it still tired his opponent's arms and he was stalling for a rest. Brand gave him none, driving forward in a straight thrust that had killed people before. But he was not as fast as he could be, nor did the power of the strike drive up from his legs as much as it should have. Gormengil brushed it aside with a sweep of the twin blades, and held his ground where he stood. He was an image of supreme confidence, and once more Brand felt a cold shiver run up his spine.

"Your head will sit upon a pole next to Unferth's soon," Gormengil taunted. Then he came forward to attack again. This time he did so carefully, driving one deadly swing after another at Brand, but only one at a time, meting them out judiciously so as to preserve his strength.

Brand backed away. The rain began to fall now, no mere drizzle but a heavy torrent that fell in waves, lightened, and then came again heavier than before. Thunder rumbled with it, and a bolt of lightning slivered through the air to strike a tree on the pine-clad ridges above them.

Nothing stopped the combatants. It seemed that the whole army watched them, and no storm nor danger would force people away to seek shelter. They all knew that Brand had been injured on the battlements. They all knew Gormengil was a great fighter. And a battle unfolded before them the like of which they had never seen. For though Brand was disadvantaged, yet he always seemed to avoid the deadly blows directed at him. Though he stumbled and fell, he righted himself at the last minute. Though he swayed with dizziness, he dodged blow after blow that should have killed him. And though his knees buckled beneath him, yet still he somehow stayed on his feet and defied his opponent. The Callenor admired that, for they saw there was no give in Brand. But they knew it could not last.

Nor were they wrong. Brand knew it, and knew that it was all he could do to just defend himself. Attacking was beyond him, for he had neither the strength nor the speed. The roaring in his ears grew so loud he was not sure if it was him or if thunder rumbled continuously. But he must go on, and he *must* find a way to win.

The raven-axe whistled through the air. Brand was not quick enough. He was struck a mighty blow on his helm and toppled to the ground. Yet still he did not give up. Even as Gormengil came in for the kill, he thrust upward with his sword. The strike was fast, but his enemy was quicker. The axe whistled again, and Brand's sword was caught between one of the blades and the stabbing beak. Gormengil gave a sudden twist, and the blade was stuck fast.

Too late Brand realized what Gormengil had done, and the true purpose of the axe's beak. It was like a sword breaker. The work of the dwarves was cunning, and his sword was trapped.

Gormengil pushed both axe and sword to the ground, and then he stomped upon the blade. Great as it was, Halathrin-wrought and imbued with magic, it could not endure such force from that angle. The blade broke. The hilt was ripped from Brand's hand. A sudden light flashed, blindingly bright and lightning arced from the sky to strike a tree on the ridge. Thunder rolled across the field, and Brand's heart lurched at the loss of a weapon that was sacred to his people and that had been borne by his forefathers since the founding of the Duthgar. He felt also the shadow of death fall upon him.

Gormengil towered over him, the axe raised high. The roaring in Brand's ears rose to a crescendo. The axe whistled down, cutting for his neck, and Brand could not escape it.

But it was not in his nature to give up. His sword was broken, yet the helm he wore was Halathrin-wrought also. One final gamble he took. Tilting his head he took the full force of the blow on his helm. He felt the weight of it crashing down, and he felt his head knocked to the side. His vision faded out so that he saw nothing, yet still he drew a dagger and stabbed upward.

The blade hit something, but he did not know what. He rolled to the side, far too slow to avoid another blow, but it never came. He staggered to his feet, and his vision swam. The blackness receded, bit by bit, and he saw Gormengil before him.

But his enemy made no move to attack. He had dropped the axe and instead clamped both hands against a wound in his thigh. Even so, blood spurted and Brand knew his dagger had struck the great artery in his enemy's leg. It was a killing blow unless a tourniquet was applied immediately.

Summoning the last of his strength and trusting to luck, Brand dived and rolled. All in one motion he dropped his dagger, grabbed the haft of the axe and rose again. There he swayed, half seeing his enemy, but suddenly one stroke away from victory.

Gormengil seemed a man little given to showing his emotions, but fear and shock showed on his face. He was going to die. Victory had turned to defeat, and all his dreams were ash.

Brand had little liking for him, but he could not just watch him die. Still less did he wish to strike him down with the axe, though he knew Gormengil would not hesitate to do the same. But he was not Gormengil, and though what he was about to do could prove costly, he saw no other choice.

Brand lowered the axe, resting it upon the ground and leaning on it like a walking stick to keep his balance. "Quickly!" he called. "Get this man a tourniquet!"

For a single moment, nothing happened. All that moved was the rain falling in sheets. Then men were running to the tent. There would be cloth in there, or clothes, or rope. Something to try to stop Gormengil bleeding out where he stood.

But even as the men moved the air sizzled. It was a strange sound, and frightening. The hair on Brand's neck stood on end. Light flashed near the tent as a bolt of lightning hit the ground and the crack of thunder came with it like a blow.

Warriors reeled away. Dirt flew into the air. Steam hissed and spurted, and Brand watched, stunned, as a figure formed amid the roiling turmoil. It was the Trickster. And as she strode forward Brand heard a moan from his left. It was Horta.

But the Trickster ignored him. She ignored everyone. Like a queen she walked, her gaze on Gormengil only. And when she reached him, she placed a hand upon his shoulder. Only then did she deign to look at anyone else and speak.

"Thus I claim what is owed to me," she said to Horta. "The chieftain of the Callenor." And then her gaze turned to Brand. "Even if it is not what I sought."

She flung up her arm, and lightning sizzled again, stabbing up from her fingertips into the cloud-dark sky. Light flashed, searingly bright, and when Brand opened his eyes once more neither the goddess nor Gormengil were there.

Brand leaned wearily on the axe and gazed around him while the rain fell. Of Horta, there was no sign. Had the goddess taken him, or had he fled? Probably the latter.

"Well," Brand said, "the fight is done, and I am the victor. Will you honor the pledge to let us go freely back to the fortress?"

One of Gormengil's captains stepped a few paces forward. He was older than the others, with a short gray beard. He had the look of a lord about him, but most if not all Gormengil's captains would have been.

"We of the Callenor have as much honor as the Duthenor. You are free to go."

Brand nodded in acknowledgement. But he made no move to step away.

"There's much that the Callenor and Duthenor share in common. Not just honor, nor our distant ancestors."

The lord looked at him curiously. "So it is said, and it is said with truth."

"For instance," Brand continued, "our laws are mostly the same, especially those that govern the rights of the people, and succession to the chieftainship. So much alike, that I believe in challenging Gormengil to a duel and then defeating him … Perhaps I have a claim to the chieftainship of the Callenor tribe. Is it so?"

There was a long silence, and the rain fell about them almost unnoticed.

"There are some who would say so," the lord answered carefully.

"Let me be clear," Brand said. "I may have a claim to the chieftainship, but I would never try to enforce it. In truth, I cannot. But I have heard that Gormengil was the only true heir. And he is gone, leaving your tribe leaderless. So, I propose this. Take me as your chieftain, if even only temporarily. In that way we can avoid war and bloodshed amongst ourselves. But what happens between us is only a part of what is afoot." He paused then, thinking his next words through carefully. About them, the rain began to diminish.

"You have seen the goddess. She took Gormengil, but she is not alone. Horta, whom you know, serves her and her like. And there is now, even as we speak, an army marching toward us. You have only my word for this, but I give it with honor. I speak the truth. Enemies gather. Not just of the Duthenor but of the Callenor. And of the world as we know it. Lands and realms will fall before them. Ours will just be the first. But, perhaps, we can stop it. If we cease our own battle and unite. What do you say?"

If the silence had been long before, it was longer now. The lords regarded him with troubled eyes. But the gray-bearded warrior paid them no attention. His gaze on Brand only, he eventually shrugged and then knelt.

"I believe you. You are a man of courage and strength. If I am a judge of men, you are worthy. And the truth of your warning is in your eyes. I will serve you."

This swayed the others. They too knelt and offered their service.

Brand raised the raven-axe in salute. But as he did so, his gaze fell to his own broken sword. The sight of it weighed heavily upon him, and he remembered the prophecy of the witch in the swamp. If she was right, there was more yet to come.

Epilogue

This was no desert land. It was green, and bird and tree and animal were all different. But no matter the changes to the landscape as they marched, one thing would remain unalterable. Warfare. The stronger, the better trained, the smarter led would prevail over the weaker.

Wena turned his head from side to side and surveyed the army he led. Footmen were the greater part, but there were charioteers too. Swords hung at the sides of men. Spears were in their hands. And the bright look of battle-lust shone eagerly in their eyes. They marched to war, and a cloud of dust rose behind them. Soon, fear would press ahead of them, and the enemy would tremble.

The long days of marching were good. It brought them closer to battle and victory. But night was better, for in his dreams the long-foretold god came to him and urged him forward with promises of glory.

And of late, Wena had begun to hear Char-harash in his waking moments. Even now, he heard the god's voice whisper in his mind. *Come to me, my children. Hasten! A new day is dawning. The old gods will rule again, and the Kar-ahn-hetep will conquer the world!*

Wena strode ahead, and his army followed after him.

Thus ends *The Crimson Lord*. The Dark God Rises trilogy will continue in book three, *The Dark God*, where Brand must face his greatest enemies ever: not just men, nor sorcerers … but gods.

Meanwhile, learn some of Brand's history in *Fate of Kings,* the complete Son of Sorcery trilogy.

FATE OF KINGS

THE COMPLETE SON OF SORCERY TRILOGY

Amazon lists millions of titles, and I'm glad you discovered this one. But if you'd like to know when I release a new book, instead of leaving it to chance, sign up for my newsletter. I'll send you an email on publication.

Yes please! – Go to www.homeofhighfantasy.com and sign up.

No thanks – I'll take my chances.

Dedication

There's a growing movement in fantasy literature. Its name is noblebright, and it's the opposite of grimdark.

Noblebright celebrates the virtues of heroism. It's an old-fashioned thing, as old as the first story ever told around a smoky campfire beneath ancient stars. It's storytelling that highlights courage and loyalty and hope for the spirit of humanity. It recognizes the dark – the dark in us all, and the dark in the villains of its stories. It recognizes death, and treachery and betrayal. But it dwells on none of these things.

I dedicate this book, such as it is, to that which is noblebright. And I thank the authors before me who held the torch high so that I could see the path: J.R.R. Tolkien, C.S. Lewis, Terry Brooks, David Eddings, Susan Cooper, Roger Taylor and many others. I salute you.

And, for a time, I too will hold the torch as high as I can.

Appendix: Encyclopedic Glossary

Note: the glossary of each book in this series is individualized for that book alone. Additionally, there is often historical material provided in its entries for people, artifacts and events that are not included in the main text.

Many races dwell in Alithoras. All have their own language, and though sometimes related to one another the changes sparked by migration, isolation and various influences often render these tongues unintelligible to each other.

The ascendancy of Halathrin culture, combined with their widespread efforts to secure and maintain allies against elug incursions, has made their language the primary means of communication between diverse peoples.

For instance, a merchant of Cardoroth addressing a Duthenor warrior would speak Halathrin, or a simplified version of it, even though their native speeches stem from the same ancestral language.

This glossary contains a range of names and terms. Many are of Halathrin origin, and their meaning is provided. The remainder derive from native tongues and are obscure, so meanings are only given intermittently.

Often, Duthenor names and Halathrin elements are combined. This is especially so for the aristocracy. Few other tribes of men had such long-term friendship with the immortal Halathrin as the Duthenor, and though in this relationship they lost some of their natural culture, they gained nobility and knowledge in return.

List of abbreviations:

Cam. Camar

Comb. Combined

Cor. Corrupted form

Duth. Duthenor

Hal. Halathrin

Kir. Kirsch

Prn. Pronounced

Alithoras: *Hal.* "Silver land." The Halathrin name for the continent they settled after leaving their own homeland. Refers to the extensive river and lake systems they found and their wonder at the beauty of the land.

Anast Dennath: *Hal.* "Stone mountains." Mountain range in northern Alithoras. Source of the river known as the Careth Nien that forms a natural barrier between the lands of the Camar people and the Duthenor and related tribes. Also the location of the Dweorhrealm, the underground stronghold of the dwarven nation.

Aranloth: *Hal.* "Noble might." A lòhren of ancient heritage and friend to Brand.

Arnhaten: *Kir.* "Disciples." Servants of a magician. One magician usually has many disciples, but only some of these are referred to as "inner door." Inner door disciples receive a full transmission of the master's knowledge. The remainder do not, but they continue to strive to earn the favor of their master. Until they do, they are dispensable.

Black Talon: The sign of Unferth's house. Appears on his banner and is his personal emblem. Legend claims the founder of the house in ancient days had the power to transform into a raven. Disguised in this form, and trusted as a magical being, he gave misinformation and ill-advice to the enemies of his people.

Brand: *Duth.* "Torch." An exiled Duthenor tribesman and adventurer. Appointed by the former king of Cardoroth to serve as regent for Prince Gilcarist. By birth, he is the rightful chieftain of the Duthenor people. However, Unferth the Usurper overthrew his father, killing both him and his wife. Brand, only a youth at the time, swore an oath of vengeance. That oath has long slept, but it is not forgotten, either by Brand or the usurper.

Breath of the dragon: An ancient saying of Letharn origin. They believed the magic of dragons was the preeminent magic in the world because dragons were creatures able to travel through time. Dragon's breath is known to mean fire, the destructive face of their nature. But the Letharn also believed dragons could breathe mist. This was the healing face of their nature. And the mist-breath of a dragon was held to be able to change destinies and bring good luck. To "ride the dragon's breath" meant that for a period a person was a focal point of time and destiny. The Kar-ahn-hetep peoples hold similar beliefs.

Brodruin: *Duth.* "Dark river." A lord of the Duthgar.

Bruidiger: *Duth.* "Blessed blade." A Norvinor warrior. Brand's father once saved his father's life during a hunting expedition.

Brunhal: *Duth.* "Hallowed woman." Former chieftainess of the Duthenor. Wife to Drunn, former chieftain of the Duthenor. Mother to Brand. According to Duthenor custom, a chieftain and chieftainess co-ruled.

Callenor: *Duth.* One of several tribes closely related to the Duthenor. This one inhabits lands immediately west of the Duthgar.

Camar: *Cam. Prn.* Kay-mar. A race of interrelated tribes that migrated in two main stages. The first brought them to the vicinity of Halathar, homeland of the immortal Halathrin; in the second, they separated and established cities along a broad stretch of eastern Alithoras. Related to the Duthenor, though far more distantly than the Callenor.

Cardoroth: *Cor. Hal. Comb. Cam.* A Camar city, often called Red Cardoroth. Some say this alludes to the red granite commonly used in the construction of its buildings, others that it refers to a prophecy of destruction.

Careth Nien: *Hal. Prn.* Kareth ny-en. "Great river." Largest river in Alithoras. Has its source in the mountains
209

of Anast Dennath and runs southeast across the land before emptying into the sea. It was over this river (which sometimes freezes along its northern stretches) that the Camar and other tribes migrated into the eastern lands. Much later, Brand came to the city of Cardoroth by one of these ancient migratory routes.

Char-harash: *Kir.* "He who destroys by flame." Most exalted of the emperors of the Kirsch, and a magician of great power.

Dragon of the Duthgar: The banner of the chieftains of the Duthenor. Legend holds that an ancient forefather of the line slew a dragon and ate its heart. Dragons are seen by the Duthenor as creatures of ultimate evil, but the consuming of their heart is reputed to pass on wisdom and magic.

Drunn: *Duth.* "Man of secrets." Former chieftain of the Duthenor. Husband to Brunhal and father to Brand.

Duthenor: *Duth. Prn.* Dooth-en-or. "The people." A single tribe (or less commonly a group of closely related tribes melded into a larger people at times of war or disaster) who generally live a rustic and peaceful lifestyle. They are breeders of cattle and herders of sheep. However, when need demands they are bold warriors – men and women alike. Currently ruled by a usurper who murdered Brand's parents. Brand has sworn an oath to overthrow the tyrant and avenge his parents.

Duthgar: *Duth.* "People spear." The name is taken to mean "the land of the warriors who wield spears."

Elù-haraken: *Hal.* "The shadowed wars." Long ago battles in a time that is become myth to the Duthenor and Camar tribes. A great evil was defeated, though prophecy foretold it would return.

Elùgai: *Hal. Prn.* Eloo-guy. "Shadowed force." The sorcery of an elùgroth.

Garvengil: *Duth.* "Warrior of the woods." A lord of the Duthgar.

God-king: See Char-harsh.

Gormengil: *Duth.* "Warrior of the storm." Nephew of Unferth. Rightful heir to the Callenor chieftainship.

Halathrin: *Hal.* "People of Halath." A race named after an honored lord who led an exodus of his people to the land of Alithoras in pursuit of justice, having sworn to defeat a great evil. They are human, though of fairer form, greater skill and higher culture than ordinary men. They possess a unity of body, mind and spirit that enables insight and endurance beyond the native races of Alithoras. Said to be immortal, but killed in great numbers during their conflicts in ancient times with the evil they sought to destroy. Those conflicts are collectively known as the Shadowed Wars.

Haldring: *Duth.* "White blade – a sword that flashes in the sun." A shield-maiden. Killed in the first great battle between the forces of Brand and the usurper.

High Way: An ancient road longer than the Duthgar, but well preserved in that land. Probably of Letharn origin and used to speed troops to battle.

Horta: *Kir.* "Speech of the acacia tree." It is believed among the Kar-ahn-hetep that the acacia tree possesses magical properties that aid discourse between the realms of men and gods. Horta is a name that recurs among families noted for producing elite magicians.

Hralfling: *Duth.* "The shower of sparks off two sword blades striking." An elderly lord of the Callenor.

Hruidgar: *Duth.* "Ashwood spear." A Duthenor hunter.

Immortals: See Halathrin.

Karak: The dwarven rune for victory. Famous in the Shadowed Wars, where also the dwarves came to prominence for the crafting of superb weapons and armor.

Kar-ahn-hetep: *Kir.* "The children of the thousand stars." A race of people that vied for supremacy in ancient times with the Letharn. Their power was ultimately broken, their empire destroyed. But a residual population survived and defied outright annihilation by their conquerors. They believe their empire will one day rise again to rule the world. The kar-ahn element of their name means the "thousand stars" but also "the lights that never die."

Kar-fallon: *Kir.* "Death city." A great city of the Kar-ahn-hetep that served as their principal religious focus. Their magician-priests conducted the great rites of their nation in its sacred temples.

Kar-karmun: *Kir.* "Death-life – the runes of life and death." A means of divination that distills the wisdom and worldview of the Kar-ahn-hetep civilization.

Kirsch: See Kar-ahn-hetep.

Kurik: A wizard-priest of the Letharn. Cousin to the emperor, and ruler and protector of a large military district.

Laigern: *Cam.* "Storm-tossed sea." Head guard of a merchant caravan.

Letharn: *Hal.* "Stone raisers. Builders." A race of people that in antiquity conquered most of Alithoras. Now, only faint traces of their civilization endure.

Light of Kar-fallon: See Char-harash.

Lòhren: *Hal. Prn.* Ler-ren. "Knowledge giver – a counselor." Other terms used by various nations include wizard, druid and sage.

Lòhrengai: *Hal. Prn.* Ler-ren-guy. "Lòhren force." Enchantment, spell or use of mystic power. A manipulation and transformation of the natural energy inherent in all things. Each use takes something from the user. Likewise, some part of the transformed energy infuses them. Lòhrens use it sparingly, elùgroths indiscriminately.

Lord of the Ten Armies: See Char-harash.

Magic: Mystic power. See lòhrengai and elùgai.

Norhanu: *Kir.* "Serrated blade." A psychoactive herb.

Norvinor: *Duth.* One of several tribes closely related to the Duthenor. This one inhabits lands west of the Callenor.

Olbata: *Kir.* "Silence of the desert at night." An inner door disciple of Horta.

Pennling Palace: A fortress in the Duthgar. Named after an ancient hero of the Duthenor. In truth, constructed by the Letharn and said to be haunted by the spirits of the dead. At certain nights, especially midwinter and midsummer, legend claims the spirits are visible manning the walls and fighting a great battle.

Pennling Path: Etymology obscure. Pennling was an ancient hero of the Duthenor. Some say he built the road in the Duthgar known as the High Way. This is not true, but one legend holds that he traveled all its length in one night on a milk-white steed to confront an attacking army by himself. It is said that his ghost may yet be seen racing along the road on his steed when the full moon hangs above the Duthgar.

Ruler of the Thousand Stars: See Char-harash.

Runes of Life and Death: See Kar-karmun.

Shadowed wars: See Elù-haraken.

Shemfal: *Kir.* "Cool shadows gliding over the hot waste – dusk." One of the greater gods of the Kar-ahn-hetep. Often depicted as a mighty man, bat winged and bat headed. Ruler of the underworld. Given a wound in battle with other gods that does not heal and causes him to limp.

Shenti: A type of kilt worn by the Kar-ahn-hetep.

Shorty: A former Durlindrath (chief bodyguard of the king of Cardoroth). Friend to Brand. His proper name is Lornach.

Sighern: *Duth.* "Battle leader." A youth of the Duthgar.

Su-sarat: *Kir.* "The serpent that lures." One of the greater gods of the Kar-ahn-hetep. Her totem is the desert puff adder that lures prey by flicking either its tongue or tail. Called also the Trickster. It was she who gave the god Shemfal his limp.

Tanata: *Kir.* "Stalker of the desert at night." A disciple of Horta.

Taingern: *Cam.* "Still sea," or "calm waters." A former Durlindrath (chief bodyguard of the king of Cardoroth). Friend to Brand.

Tinwellen: *Cam.* "Sun of the earth – gold." Daughter of a prosperous merchant of Cardoroth.

Unferth: *Duth.* "Hiss of arrows." The name is sometimes interpreted to mean "whispered counsels that lead to war." Usurper of the chieftainship of the Duthenor. Rightful chieftain of the Callenor.

Ùhrengai: *Hal. Prn.* Er-ren-guy. "Original force." The primordial force that existed before substance or time.

Vorbald: *Duth.* "Wolf warrior." A great warrior among the Callenor.

Wena: *Kir.* "The kestrel that hovers." Leader of a Kar-ahn-hetep army.

Wizard: See lòhren.

Wizard-priest: The priests of the Letharn. Possessors of mighty powers of magic. Forerunners to the order of lòhrens.

About the author

I'm a man born in the wrong era. My heart yearns for faraway places and even further afield times. Tolkien had me at the beginning of *The Hobbit* when he said, ". . . one morning long ago in the quiet of the world . . ."

Sometimes I imagine myself in a Viking mead-hall. The long winter night presses in, but the shimmering embers of a log in the hearth hold back both cold and dark. The chieftain calls for a story, and I take a sip from my drinking horn and stand up . . .

Or maybe the desert stars shine bright and clear, obscured occasionally by wisps of smoke from burning camel dung. A dry gust of wind marches sand grains across our lonely campsite, and the wayfarers about me stir restlessly. I sip cool water and begin to speak.

I'm a storyteller. A man to paint a picture by the slow music of words. I like to bring faraway places and times to life, to make hearts yearn for something they can never have, unless for a passing moment.

Made in the USA
Middletown, DE
18 April 2020